Look What You Made Me Do

Horror Stories Inspired by the Music of Taylor Swift

Sobelo Books

Sobelo Books

Copyright © 2026 by Sobelo Books LLC
Individual works copyright © 2026 by their respective authors.

All rights reserved.

No part of this publication may be reproduced, distributed, or transmitted in any form or by any means, including photocopying, recording, or other electronic or mechanical methods, without the prior written permission of the publisher, except as permitted by U.S. copyright law. For permission requests, contact lucas@sobelobooks.com.

The story, all names, characters, and incidents portrayed in this production are fictitious. No identification with actual persons (living or deceased), places, buildings, and products is intended or should be inferred.

NO AI TRAINING: Without in any way limiting the author's [and publisher's] exclusive rights under copyright, any use of this publication to "train" generative artificial intelligence (AI) technologies to generate text is expressly prohibited.

Cover Art by Chris Panatier

Cover Wrap Designed by Drew Huff

Edited by L.P. Hernandez and L.C. Marino

ISBN (paperback): 978-1-965389-17-1
ISBN (hardcover): 978-1-965389-29-4
ISBN (ebook): 978-1-965389-16-4

First edition, 2026

Praise for Look What You Made Me Do

"These stories are so great we decided to publish them." – **Sobelo Books**

"I love nothing more than editing short stories and this anthology is full of 'em." – **L.P. Hernandez**, author of *In The Valley of the Headless Men*, *No Gods, Only Chaos,* and *Sky Lights*

"What he said." – **L.C. Marino**, author of *The Haunting of the Whispering House* series and coauthor of the hit survival thriller series *Only Darkness Remains*

Contents

Foreword	1
Cardigan	5
Sweet Nothing	23
I Knew You Were Trouble	37
Ivy	53
Picture to Burn	71
Marjorie	85
I Look In People's Windows	99
No Body, No Crime	113
Better Than Revenge	119
Look What You Made Me Do	135
Shake It Off	149
Vigilante Shit	165
Who's Afraid of Little Old Me?	187

Foreword

By Stephanie Gagnon

"I don't know, it's some kind of Dracula conference, or something," a girl says into her phone as she walks by me. There's a Sharpied #13 drawn on her hand, the Swiftie giveaway, if it weren't for her glittering pink ensemble. It's the summer of 2023 and Taylor Swift announced her Eras tour, a 3-hour spectacle encompassing 10 albums and their corresponding visual worlds, (obviously this girl's destination.) I'm standing in the lobby of the Sheraton at Station Square in Pittsburgh, and I'm here for the "Dracula conference."

StokerCon, the annual gathering of the Horror Writers' Association, happened to coincide with the Pittsburgh leg of Taylor's concert tour. This overlap resulted in quite the striking clash of aesthetics at the hotel. You could walk into the lobby bathroom and encounter someone in a glittering lavender dress applying lip gloss next to someone with a blood-splattered Ghostface tee. Two fandoms, both alike in dignity, forced to share a hotel for a summer weekend. And as someone who walks the line between both worlds, as a horror fan and a Swiftie, I'd argue that they share more in common than you might think.

I started listening to Taylor around the time her self-titled debut album was released in 2006. Listening to "Teardrops on My Guitar" made me feel like someone had read from my own diary. It was a song about teen heartbreak and unrequited love, and one that wasn't talking down to the listener. It met me exactly where I was. As she matured, so did the themes of her music; the relationships gained new complex layers, but the resonance remained as I matured with her and found my life also gaining new complexities and nuances.

"Really? What does any of this have to do with horror?", you might be asking yourself. It's a fair question. Taylor Swift and horror don't seem to be the most obvious of bedfellows. Swifties might point you toward her 2017 album Reputation, aesthetically the darkest in her catalog. Reputation was released after an uncharacteristically quiet period from Swift, a social media self-exile after public backlash. Singles from the album dropped without the usual promotion cycle "there will be no explanation, only reputation." The music video for "Look What You Made Me Do" opens on a gravestone reading "Here Lies Taylor Swift's Reputation" where an undead Taylor bursts through the dirt and crawls her way out of the grave only to turn around and bury an old version of herself in her place. Using horror visuals to communicate themes around reinvention that she would return to time and again.

Though Reputation is the era that most obviously adopts horror visuals, there are dark themes throughout her discography. Even in 1989, an album that marked her official pivot from country to pop, she takes aim at the obsession around her dating life in "Blank Space." A satirical song where she embraces this serial-dating maneater persona. She leans into this in the music video where we see her go from the girl of your dreams to an unhinged, mascara-stained wreck slashing tires. She's a nightmare dressed like a daydream.

It's not limited to those either. She is the tragic ghostly narrator haunting the restaurant in right where you left me. She is an avenging angel in no body, no crime. She is the feral force in Who's Afraid of Little Old Me. She drapes herself in the Gothic throughout the sister albums folklore and evermore. Even lines like, "I'm getting tired even for a Phoenix, always risin' from the ashes, mending all her gashes" hearken visuals of weary final girls gearing up to fight their presumed-dead foes in yet another franchise installment. Her lyricism is rife with the drama and catharsis that fans look for in their horror stories. She buries hatchets, but she keeps maps of where she put them. Yes, she's Miss Americana, a pop princess, but one that offers plenty for horror fans to enjoy.

And so Look What You Made Me Do is digging up the grave to create horror stories within the world of Taylor's music. These stories are playing in the sandbox of her lyrics, constructing haunted houses, crazed nightmares and bloody delights from the well of her words. Don't discount the potential for horror just because it's written in pink gel pen.

Stephanie Gagnon

Cardigan

By Neil McRobert

Folks round here think my daddy was a bad man.

Course, they're right. He was a drunk and a cheat, in cards as well as marriage. More than once he lost a whole week's wages before he even got out of the foundry gates. Squandered our livelihood chasing games of pitch and toss that got away from him, cos he was too dumb and proud to know when he was beat. Then he'd come home and whale on Ma for having the temerity to complain. When I was eight years old, he split my head for waking him from a Sunday hangover. Just grabbed a hunk of pine from the fireplace and let me have it between the eyes. Sloped back to bed, leaving Gran to hustle me to the emergency room with a promise to say that I'd fallen from the oak in the yard.

I hated my daddy. He was a miserable, small kind of monster.

But he didn't kill those girls.

On that score, the folks around here are dead wrong. As wrong as those girls are dead.

Why am I so sure? Well, that's the part you may not believe.

What's the first thing you remember? For most folks it's some loose sensory fragment: the taste of cake frosting on their fourth birthday, the smack of a parent's hand, or a rough sandpaper kiss from the family dog.

My first memory is darkness. Not the scary blue-black of a midnight bedroom, but a comforting cocoon, both narrow and endless. I blend into it, past any sense of my own edges. Darkness isn't even the right word, 'cuz there's no sight for me there. No smell, touch or taste either. There's just sound, or some dull semblance that's closer to vibration. A gentle bassline that tells me I'm safe and held.

The memory stretches out like a dream or a drug nod. Then, some no-time later, there's a change that brings me back. It's the rhythm. The drummer in my little universe has gone off the beat, slowing down for long pauses, then rushing to catch up. A mad cadence that sends everything around me into spasm.

I wait for a settling, but it only gets more hectic. Then comes the drainage, a sense of something vital flooding away, and for the first time I'm aware of limits to myself. Of *me*-ness and *other*-ness. I feel walls, soft but relentless. They push inward, downward, moving me towards an unkind purpling that grows brighter by the second, until horrifically, there's light. With my first scream building inside me, I slide out of Ma into a cruel halogen dawn.

I'm appalled by the bright and the chill and the newness, and I shriek louder as I'm handled by strange arms, as Ma recedes into the blur, taking sanctuary with her.

Why? I remember thinking, though surely, I could have had no understanding of the question. Just like I could not have known that heaving pink shape was Ma.

How could you?

Rough hands grasp me and the world spins. Something vast fills my shallow field of vision. A face, creased as badly hung wallpaper beneath a fuzz of grey, behind spectacles. In my memory I recognise myself in those reflecting lenses, though, of course, this cannot be true.

I feel the dry pressure of lips on my forehead, then the tickle of the same against my ear. These are the first words I ever hear.

"Hello child. I'm your gran, and you're my favourite."

They found the first girl in the Monongahela. A fisherman caught more than he was hoping for one brisk March morning in 1995: a corpse, naked and pale as a walleye's belly. She'd been strangled and cut, and though the river had cleansed her of evidence, enough people knew her as Wendy St. Peters that attention soon turned to Daddy. After Ma died, he'd been quite the barfly, and in the weeks before Wendy was last seen, her and Daddy had been barstool buddies down at the Old Forge on Coker Road. He'd brought her home a time or two, much to Gran's distaste. She didn't like "loose women," certainly not those young enough to be her granddaughter.

Wendy was always nice to me though. I was sad that she died, thought at ten years old sadness passes quickly.

The policemen asked Daddy questions, but they couldn't stick anything on him. Plenty of people orbited Wendy St Peters. She was a friendly girl.

"Too damned friendly," Gran said.

The following October a jogger stumbled over Carly Kells in the woods east of town, and all hell broke loose in our little corner of heaven.

Policemen practically beat our door down. There were four of them and the biggest one spat in Daddy's face when he cuffed him.

"Careful man!" His partner nodded toward me and Gran.

"What's she gonna say?" the big man scorned. "Her son's a goddamn monster, ain't that right Mrs. Dorty?"

Gran said nothing. Her face stayed granite as they led Daddy from the house."Hey Mama," he slurred. "I done nothing. Tell 'em Mama." His feet shuffled for purchase on the linoleum.

Daddy was a ghost through the window of the cruiser. He shouted for her, but she only looked on, a slightly steeper frown than usual on her always grim face.

"Come on, August," she said, landing a papery hand on my shoulder. "Let's go inside."

Even with the front door closed, I could still hear Daddy's cries.

Gran cooked us up some soup and we watched television.

Ma hated Gran, and the feeling was mutual. I remember all of it, or as much as anyone can about anything. I'm not saying I have perfect recall, like that detective on the TV, but I know enough.

When we left the hospital, it was Gran who carried me to the car. Ma trailed after her like a lost sheep, bleating about how I was *her* baby. Gran mostly ignored her, just as she disregarded Ma's opinion on my name.

"I want to call him Timothy, after my brother," Ma said.

"Timothy is a weak name. August. That's what we'll call him. A good strong, earthy name for a strong boy."

When Ma protested Gran turned to Daddy. "What do you think, son? Don't you want him to bear your father's name? He was a grand, handsome man."

Daddy was three sheets on cheap rye and only grunted. Gran took that as assent, and so I came to be August Dorty. The second of my name, if you want to be a purist about it.

That drama played out whilst I rocked in a crib by the fireplace, two days old and tracing the blurry contours of the sitting room. One room in a house I'd call home for these forty years, but at the time it was my whole world. I remember the green tartan blanket that Gran had swaddled me in, the rough wool chafing my tender flesh. Ma insisted on using the cotton that she'd bought from the store, but Gran disdained that too.

"That's family tartan from the old country. The Docherty tartan. It has heritage."

It scratched terribly, but I cried whenever Ma swapped it for the softer cotton. I was angry at Ma, always angry. She'd turned me out of the safe, warm place inside her, and I would never forgive. Weeks after I was born, when she'd stopped limping, and getting out of a chair wasn't so hard, I still wanted her to suffer.

So, I cried at the cotton and gurgled happily at the burning wool.

At night I'd lie in my crib at the foot of the bed Ma shared with Daddy. It was the one place where Gran never interfered.

"The workings of a marriage are nothing to do with me," she'd say.

"Funny," Ma complained in the lamplight. "She never has any problems sticking her oar into our workings the rest of the time. But when the baby is crying at three in the morning, that's when she thinks we need privacy."

Daddy would grunt, scowl, or just seethe in silence. Sometimes he'd snap back that it was his mother's house, and she could do as she wanted.

"But you promised we'd have a place of our own by now. It's been years, Donny. What kind of marriage is this?"

"The kind we can afford, now shut up and let me sleep."

Sometimes Ma would keep pushing and Daddy would get louder. Eventually I'd hear the sharp crack of a palm against flesh.

After that, silence. And a colder dark than the one I still longed for.

Carly Kells lived two streets over. Her Daddy worked with mine at the foundry and she babysat me on the rare occasion Gran was busy. She was a pretty brunette, nice enough, though her breath smelled of cigarettes, and sometimes she'd tickle me long enough that I peed my pants.

I wasn't as saddened by her death as I was by Wendy's.

Carly had similar bruising around her neck and the same pattern of incisions in her flesh, but her body told the policemen much more than Wendy's. When the flesh under her fingernails was eventually tested it matched the scratches in Daddy's back. There were signs of roughness downstairs, and they matched that to Daddy too. That lab stuff is what nailed him at the trial, but in the court of public opinion, it was just more seasoning in the stew. People were already convinced he'd killed her. He'd been seen around Furnace with Carly in his truck, and what on earth would a thirty-nine-year-old man want with a seventeen-year-old girl, if not *that*?

Gran had warned him to drop her.

"She's too young for you Donny, and she's loose. I never liked letting her near the boy."

"She's okay," he'd say. "A man's gotta have some fun. I work hard enough."

"Get yourself a nice girl," Gran repeated, over and over. "A nice, quiet girl who knows her place."

"Nice ain't all that fun," he'd grin.

I bet he wished he'd listened to her when the policemen took him. He swore he had nothing to do with Carly, or Wendy for that matter. But they had enough on him to get a warrant, and before we knew it there were men on our land with shovels and chemistry sets.

Gran watched them dig from the back porch, *tsking* when they dug up her roses. She grew beautiful roses. Seeing them ruined made her mouth sour, but that was the only chink she let show. The rest of the time she was stony as ever. Even when they started bringing up the girls.

Ten of them. Ten bodies buried on our land. All females. Aged fourteen to nineteen. Except the one under the roses.

Except for Ma.

I watched three of the burials from the porch, where I sat in my bouncer, goggling at the bright day and laughing as the dirt flew. I can't have been any older than two or three when I saw the last one go into the ground. After that, I guess there was the worry that I'd be old enough to understand what I was privy to.

When you're young, they assume you know nothing.

I've never understood how I remember so well, and until recently, I've never really cared. Was I just made different, or maybe everyone is like me, but they forget as they go? Also, seeing and understanding are different things. I saw lots, far more than Ma, Daddy and Gran realised when they popped me down in the corner of rooms like a table ornament. But I don't think I grasped the truth of it, the meaning. That came later, I think, when I looked back from an older vantage.

It's confusing.

Perhaps I made it up to explain me to myself. Is my mind feeding me false signals?

I'm not sure. But I don't think so.

Their screaming rings too real in my head.

I never liked school. It was an unkind place to me. But beyond the everyday cruelty of the classroom, there's what happens when your daddy is arrested for killing two hand counts of young girls in your town. That ratcheted things up a fair bit for sure.

It wasn't much better for Gran either. When it comes down to it, most adults are just kids wrapped in more skin, and she was subject to just as many whispers and squint-eyed stares as me. What kind of woman raises a man who can do *that?* people wondered, sometimes out loud.

'Course, I don't truly blame our neighbours. Daddy was an unpleasant man, and if the police said he did it, and the jury up in Harrisburg said he did it, and most importantly, the people on Channel 8 said he did it, then who are the good citizens of Furnace to argue?

If anyone had doubts as to the mortal guilt of Donald S. Dorty, not one of them spoke up at his trial. Not even Gran. According to the clippings in our scrapbook, Daddy cried out for her to save him, but she watched calmly as her only son was led away, wailing, to begin his long, lonely wait on the Row at Rockview.

In the end he didn't have to wait too long. He got the needle on January 2nd, 1999, when I was almost fourteen. If it hadn't been for what that perv Heidnik did to those women in his basement up in Philly, Daddy would have gone down in history as the last person to be executed in the state of Pennsylvania.

Gran was dry-eyed for that too. There's a photograph of her leaving Rockview after it was done. She's wrapped up in her cardigan—thick wool gathered like a goitre round her neck—and she's staring straight down the camera. The flash gleams off her glasses and if you were generous-minded, you could think she's in tears. But she isn't.

Betty Dorty was never one for crying or whining. And she got very impatient with those who did.

Very impatient.

I was no more than a year old when Gran took Ma down the basement. There was a nasty atmosphere soaked into everything that day, 'cuz Ma had given Daddy an especially hard time the night before. She'd ended up crying about how much she hated living here, how she loathed *that mother of yours*, who couldn't even let her raise her own child in peace.

"There's something wrong with her," Ma cried. "She gives me the shivers."

"Don't say anything else about my mother."

"Oh, why don't you just go sleep in her bed Donny? Tuck up next to her nice and tight, that's what she wants after all."

"I'm warning you, woman." Daddy's voice dropped low. I heard the threat from my crib. Me, who had never met a growling beast, I understood the danger.

Ma didn't hear it. She said she'd be gone by the end of the week, unless Daddy found them somewhere else to live. And I'd be going with her.

Hearing this, I began to cry.

Gran must've heard everything, too. The walls were like crepe in that house.

Next afternoon Daddy was pulling a double shift and Ma was busy packing a bag. "Just in case," she kept whispering.

She'd placed me on the bed beside it, where I was entertaining myself by gumming a cheap nylon blouse and watching the dust dance in the thick afternoon light. I could feel the tension in the house, and I don't think that's 'cos I'm special; babies always seem well tuned to emotional harmonics.

Gran's voice came muffled from beneath us. "Girl, come down here, I need a hand."

"Jesus wept!" Ma groaned and threw a handful more clothes into the bag.

"GIRL!"

With a snarl, Ma lifted me and stormed to the basement stairs.

"What?"

"Just get down here girl, I can't do this myself. It's heavy."

"I've got August."

"Well, leave him up there, you'll only be a tick."

Ma started down the stairs. "I'm not leaving my baby alone Betty. This is why I don't trust you with him. And will you stop calling me *girl*, I have a damn name, it's–"

She didn't get any further. As Ma stepped into the damp bowel-space of the house, the hammer came down with a single hollow thud.

Gran plucked me from Ma's arms before I could hit the ground. She buried me in her shoulder, the wirelike strands of her cardigan rubbing against my face.

I didn't cry.

She placed me on the bench in the middle of the room and went to work. I'd recently learned to roll over, and I did – whether by accident or intent, I'm not sure.

But I saw everything.

How Ma shook and jittered in the hardpacked dirt. How Gran wrapped narrow fingers around her neck and pushed down, applying every ounce of her sparrow weight to collapsing Ma's airwaves.

How she took a box cutter and carved the same words that would be later found on Wendy and Carly's bodies, and all the other women unearthed like a spoiled harvest from our land.

HOOR.

LOOSE.

'Course, I wasn't old enough to read them yet. But I watched everything. And I learned.

I learned lots of things that day, but most of all I found out that Gran loved me more than anyone.

"Take him away from me?" she hissed at Ma's corpse. "Not a chance in heaven girl. He's my favourite."

So yeah, I assumed Ma was buried with the rest. Where else would she be? Gran only started leaving them other places 'cuz she got too old to dig.

She killed five more by the time I was in middle school. That's not even counting Wendy and Carly. Six people went into the ground between her rosebushes, but ten came out. The policemen agreed that several of the bodies were much older and, as I found out later, Gran put those four bodies in the ground back in the sixties, each of them a young woman, a *loose hoor* who got a little bit too close to her grand, handsome husband.

August Dorty the First was quite the ladies' man, it seems. Daddy too. That's why she started up again, two decades after Grandpa August's death, 'cuz Daddy started in with those same low women.

Women like that weren't fit for her husband, and certainly not for her son.

She would whisper this story to them as they rattled and choked under her hands.

How do I know?

'Cuz I watched.

I'd know when she was readying herself. Whichever girl Daddy was hanging around would get an invitation to the house, always when Daddy was on a late shift or out drinking.

Or *hooring*, Gran would say, with a smack of distaste.

Usually I was the bait, the sweet, quiet, motherless child in need of a babysitter. A burden to an old lady in need of a night off.

The girl would come, and we'd play fire trucks or the-floor-is-lava, and at some point in the evening Gran would get her near the basement door and with a shove, the girl would end up at the bottom. The lucky ones were knocked cold in the fall.

One screamed like a kettle until my Gran took the hammer to her.

The screamer was the first one I watched since Ma. I was old enough to walk myself over to the basement door, and I giggled when Gran dropped the hammer, slippery with the dead girl's blood. She looked up and I just managed to duck out of sight.

After that I watched in safety, through a gap in the boards of Daddy's bedroom. I could see most of the basement, and though the shadows made it murky as unsettled pond, I could see enough.

She assumed I knew nothing.

That lasted for another ten years, until Daddy was shot up with poison and off to the angels. Though the stares continued, they were tinged with sympathy now. Gran's son was dead, my daddy was dead, and people started to see us as another kind of victim. Those who had to live in the cave with the beast.

How much did *he* know? That I've never been sure of. In all my silent spectating, not once did I see Daddy ever talk to Gran about how his women just kept up and disappearing. Maybe that speaks for itself.

It was a time of quiet for Gran. With Daddy gone there was no need to keep the *hoors* away. At least for a year or two.

See, I was a handsome boy.

And when I was old enough, she let me help.

Amber Reus was the only girl who was nice to me the year Daddy went to the Row. Being fifteen and naive, I thought she was a good girl too.

It only took one meeting for Gran to spot what I'd missed. The skirt two inches two short, the way she braided her hair, like she thought she was somebody.

Looseness.

I tried to cast her off but she was so persistent. She'd come over and kiss me and I'd do my best to keep her at bay, but I was fifteen. Like Gran said, it wasn't my fault. I'm a Dorty man.

Amber went downstairs on a late September evening. No push was needed; she was happy to help Gran bring up the laundry while she waited for me. They both thought I was out of the house. When Amber knocked on the door and Gran received her with such strange warmth in her voice, I knew enough to stay hidden in my room.

It was exciting.

Through the bedroom floor I watched Gran do her work. The hammer, the choking and the stripping of Amber's clothes. Something grew hard between me and the boards, harder than it ever had when Amber had tried to touch me.

When I reached for myself the board creaked.

Gran's head snapped up.

We stayed that way for what felt like minutes, Gran looking up, me looking down, Amber's dead eyes taking us both in from the floor. All the while my hardness pushed painfully against the pine.

It was only when Gran reached for the box cutter that I broke.

Gran must have heard my footsteps and heaven knows what she thought as I descended from the kitchen. From time to time, I've wondered if she considered the hammer.

Surely not. I was her favourite.

I paused at the bottom of the stairs, hesitant as a visitor to a foreign church.

"Hello August. I didn't know you were home."

"Can I do it?" I asked, breathless.

"Do it?"

I nodded to the box cutter in her hand.

"Can I write the words?"

She raised an eyebrow.

"I know about the words."

"Do you? And how?"

I wanted to tell her, but she wouldn't have believed me. She might have thought I was mad, and mad people can't be allowed near sharp things.

"It was on the news."

For a long moment we were as still as Amber. Gran never took her eyes from me.

Finally, she smiled and handed me the cutter.

"Show me."

So, I did. And if I wasn't as neat as she would've liked on that first try, well... all things improve with practice. Over the years I got much better. Better at spotting the loose and the hoorish, and better at branding them as such.

I was fifteen, sixteen, seventeen, and strong. Gran didn't have to drag the bodies to the quiet corners of Furnace anymore; I was plenty strong enough to dig.

And our land had been cleared. No one was coming back to search it twice.

She said I was a good boy.

I was her favourite.

Gran died in 2009. Emphysema. It gets a lot of people in Furnace. She died choking, with a rattle in her throat but her body went to the earth in pristine condition. She was a decent, proper woman. Nothing loose about Betty Dorty.

Once she was gone, I stopped doing what we did.

Mostly.

It wasn't so fun without her.

Around the same time, I met a good woman and we married. I like to think Gran would've liked her. A year ago, she had a bad fall down the basement steps and she's buried up at Mount Hope with a tidy gravestone to mark where she lays. That only seemed right, 'cuz she was a good wife. Mostly.

My boys are only two and four, but I plan to raise them to be strong Dorty men. Sometimes they make me wonder, though. I watched them slide into the world; their little faces wrinkled like spoiled fruit. They looked so very angry. I'm careful what I say around them.

As I've gotten older, I've begun to wonder more about those memories of mine. Do I really remember that warm, gentle dark inside Ma, or was I just a boy from a violent home, yearning for a safe place?

More and more I hope it's the latter, 'cuz these last few years there's another place that flickers through my head when sleep won't come. It's a vast dark, a cold dark, blacker than winter midnight. Blacker than blindness.

I think it might be the place *before*. Before Ma. Before everything.

I'm not part and parcel of *that* darkness. I'm not held. No, in that place everyone is entirely apart. And there are so many of us. There I am... I *was*... just one of a million billion islands in a sea of sightlessness.

And we are all screaming.

Do I recognise some of the voices? Amber? Ma? My wife?

Are they screaming in torment? Or is it anger?

I don't know. I don't know anything anymore. But I don't want that place to be real.

Because if it's real, and it's from *before*, what if it's also *after?*

Sweet Nothing
By Grace R. Reynolds

The world opens, a siphon for night. Lambent sunbeams slip through dust-laden blinds and I lie in bed wondering whether this will be the day the world finally ends.

I look out the window and scan the street. Dead bodies. Peeled-back eyes. Fallen corpses defiant and rotten in the yard. Sprouting weeds flourish, grow, and push through rib cages like concrete flowers.

I haven't moved or attempted to bury them. I prefer to leave them as they are, reminders that decomposition is a promise wrapped in dandelion crowns. Even now I can see a body still gripping a rusted pistol in one hand, and a rock in the other, polished and smoothed from worry in the cockcrow hour.

Some habits never die.

I never did check whether any rounds remained in that gun. I already know it's empty.

Inanis knows it, too. That black obelisk, barbaric in its passivity and observation, which floats in the sky. Together, it and I exist like binary stars yanked into orbit by the gravitational pull of this planet's last heart palpitations. A feathered pulse that flutters ever so slightly through the cosmos. I make no effort to acknowledge Inanis's presence, though. Doing so would admit defeat, and I am not yet ready to submit.

The screams of cicadas in heat claw the sky, scratching at metal window screens like the discordant melodies of life after humanity. A monotonous drone inviting me to close my eyes and sleep for a few more hours. But, as much as I would like to stay in bed for the rest of the day, and every day after that, I have appointments to keep.

And I must eat.

Something. Anything.

Today is eighty-seven days after *Zero-Day,* the day Inanis dared to flare its brilliant malice with a flash of light that dismantled the electrical grid, disrupted the earth's magnetic field, and rendered nerve cell transmissions in the brain useless. It was as quick as turning off the lights. Everything stopped, including hearts beating in the chests of every person.

Though I am still here.

I've raided all the homes on this block. During that first week alone, I scoured my neighbors' pantries for canned goods. Devoured the fresh produce before mold spores bloomed. Consumed what I could before the interred remains inside abandoned refrigerators spoiled.

I miss a lot of things. The taste of meat. The crisp bite of a red bell pepper, the way its juice would trickle down my chin like watermelon in the backyard as summer kisses my skin. One can only eat Pop-Tarts and Grape-Nuts for so long until they become completely unpalatable. They are the new hard-tack cracker of 2033. Only there's no coffee to soften them.

Cars rust. Benches bake in the sun. As I walk toward the pink stucco bungalow at the end of the street, I ignore the Graco stroller haphazardly parked in the middle of the sidewalk. I avert my eyes so I don't have to see what's underneath the canopy.

Wet and sticky with sweat, I flap the collar of my shirt and sigh. Like the smoke of a clove cigarette, I consider going to one of the corner stores later in the day. After waking up to the stink of meat again, taking a pack from behind the counter sounds great right now. Something to blunt the peaks of my jagged nerves, just to feel the smoke eddy between my lips. But not before my visit with Ms. Meredith.

My knuckles rattle on the white storm door, its chipped paint revealing the metal underneath. Its weathered nature is endearing, a sign of its fortitude.

"Mrs. Osterhausen! Ms. Meredith! It's me!"

Amidst pristine carpet and plastic-wrapped furniture, Ms. Meredith's home encapsulates a lifetime of memories in gold-framed portraits that cover the walls and nearly every flat surface. Like Mr. Osterhausen's portrait from World War II in his Army uniform. Glamour shots of their seven daughters from the 1980s. A collage of her grandchildren in their high school graduation caps hangs proudly in the TV room. I've never asked about them.

Like I know the Glock is empty, I know they're all dead.

It's not the dead grandchildren that give me pause. It's the sticky-tacky tablecloth, that green gingham pattern worn away from years of sliding cutting boards and rolling pins across it. It's the pile of Mr. Osterhausen's favorite books that Ms. Meredith left stacked on the coffee table long after his passing. It's the quiet atmosphere that this home was built on the promise to witness.

Seventy years is a long time to hold someone else's heart while entrusting them with your own. To watch someone grow into multiple versions of themselves. To experience love in all its mystery and alchemical properties transmute the two of them as they move through life together. They are—*were*—a living testament that love cannot exist in isolation.

I swallow the bitterness that bubbles up my throat.

I peer over the windowsill and see Ms. Meredith's tufts of salt and pepper curls peek through fluffy pink overgrown hydrangeas. I slide the backdoor open and step outside.

"Well, I saw him again today, Ms. Meredith. Still dead. Still holding that damn rock in his hand." I squat down on the patio. "Would you believe what's left of that asshole's eyeball was looking right at me this time? The nerve of it. I would've expected a buzzard or peckish fox to eat it by now."

Ms. Meredith says nothing, which is fine. Quiet company is better than no company.

"I'm still so mad, Ms. Meredith. I don't know what to do. What to say. I'm not sure I can forgive him just yet."

My elderly companion does not react, her face frozen in a grimace. A pill bug skitters across her knuckles, naked and exposed. I reach for her hand anyway, desperate for touch.

"I know what you'd say though. *Time heals all wounds*. That grief isn't something to get through. That it's a silent friend we must acknowledge and learn how to walk with. But you're a good woman Ms. Meredith. Always have been. Patient and kind. I can't imagine you ever being angry. So, what does that make me?" My head hangs low, shaking in disbelief. Maybe it's pointless to harp on anger, but these talks help, if only for a moment.

A grey cat emerges from the hydrangea bush, its belly swollen and pink. The cat purrs, rubs against my legs before it slumps onto the patio to stretch, languid and content in the sun. I feign a smile, but it does not reach my eyes. How can the cat bring babies into a world so full of death and sorrow?

The golden hour. Hands entwined. The warmth of skin on skin under sheets. The buzz of an alarm. Hitting the snooze button, again. Early morning showers and Eggs Benedict sandwiches. Humming in the kitchen, the reverberating sound as warm as the pour of a fresh cup of coffee. "I'll see you later," and kisses goodbye. Flashpoint. Bang. The sudden cessation of the world falling silent outside—

My cheeks flush. Tears run hot as the intensity of this memory overcomes me. Out of everyone in this town, maybe even the entire planet, how could it be I am the only one left? It is the question I've ruminated over since *it* happened. Since *he* left me, all alone, to survive the fallout.

I wish I could punch him in the face, throw that stupid rock at his eye. Cleave the husk of his heart open until the sun stops rising, because every day I open my eyes is another day I have to face a world I am afraid of and don't want to live in.

I hate him for it.

I will always hate him for it.

A monotonous clicking echoes from above. Dissonant and mechanical, its song snaps my attention to Inanis. Inanis swings low and slow above us, spinning in tight circles on its axis like the bob of a pendulum. I squint my eyes in search of the invisible string holding it there, spun together from threads of other-worldly planes like the scaffolding made by a garden orb weaver. Its obelisk form hovers ever closer, now, radiating spindles of light from its ends.

The trees shudder. Birds take flight. The ground rumbles and shakes. Pinching and expanding, Inanis is now just a sliver of black, tearing the sky asunder like the sharp point of a knife.

Extraterrestrial in both nature and form, Inanis opens.

Blocks of cement defy gravity and join together in celestial orbit around the deep gash of time and space. The maw of eternity yawns, swallowing the absence of life, and lifts that which is corporeal to new heights.

Bodies rise in the sky like flies. Articles of clothing wriggle and drop to the ground as muscle sloughs from bones. I fixate my eyes on their heads, their hair, and discernable body markings as they pass overhead, scanning the skyline to study familiar faces. I turn back, only to see Ms. Meredith's partial skeleton levitate among them, the stems of flowers and roots braided into her bones shake loose soil in clods that fall, then float, as they gravitate toward the hollow stomach of the void.

There's not enough breath in my lungs. My throat like a pinched straw, I draw breath in sharp gasps, my chest a weighted anchor.

I cannot see him.

I cannot see Henry.

I barrel through Ms. Meredith's home, the storm door shaking against its frame, as I stumble onto the sidewalk like a newborn fawn finding its legs. Heat prickles my brow as eyes follow the floating mass of neighbors and strangers hovering toward Innanis.

I break into an all-out sprint and dive into a forest of ragweed and crabgrass. Their stinging hairs needle my arms. Sap-laden kisses render my skin swollen and red. "Don't leave me. Not yet."

A cacophony of meat slapping and glass shattering rains from above. Suspended shards glint obsidian black like tiny scrying mirrors. My feet trip on unmoored slabs of stone and gravel, the thrumming of my heartbeat the only thing keeping my footsteps in tempo. My pulse quickens and reverberates, sending me into a dizzy spell that obfuscates my vision into motes of light, like looking through the small openings of a manhole.

I sit and bury my head into my knees. They look like mountain peaks, scabbed and bruised by the fragility of hope and possibility, sloping into asphalt and concrete like tectonic plates jutted above a fault line. I drag my fingers beside me, desperate to hold on to whatever part of the world will remain after this.

A thud, so small yet distinct, snaps my attention to a smooth stone on the asphalt in front of me. Familiar and foreign, I lift my head and grab the worry stone in my hand. As I turn the porous pebble over, I am both relieved and resentful it didn't crack my skull.

My fingers search the pocket of my hoodie. I pull out my phone and press the 'on' button and the screen comes to life, one last time. 3% battery. Crooked smiles and two sets of eyes flanked by crows' feet greet me, and behind them are the rolling green hills of Wicklow, Ireland, melting into the sea.

"Hi, Henry."

Soaked pants and the setting sun. It was a good trip; a memory I hoped would push out the bad and take root. A tether that would be enough to keep Henry here, with me.

It wasn't.

"It's 2:30 in the morning. Where were you?"

"Don't worry about it." Sweat reeks through Henry's clothes. His skin is flushed. Bourbon's woody scent dances in between his gums like woodlice in the bark hiding in plain sight. Like so many truths I had come to know, the undertow of amber waves fueled by his depression pulled him under again. How much does someone have to drink until they no longer see the shore?

"I don't want to fight, Jenna."

Henry falls backward onto the sofa. I want to be mad. I *am* mad. Mad enough to kick him out, but where would he go? Muscle memory betrays me as I find myself at his side searching for a way through the smoky haze of this alcohol induced episode.

A stack of sham papers on the end table flanks Henry from the right. Headlines that read *"THE END IS NEAR: DEATHS SURGE AS INANIS LOOMS CLOSER"* sits on top of others that preach *"U.S. ON THE BRINK OF WAR,"* followed by *"AMERICANS DEMAND ANSWERS: MORE THAN 50 ARRESTED AT PROTEST DEMANDING GOVERNMENT TRANSPARENCY."*

And so on. Henry swipes them off the table and buries his face into his hands.

"What's going on with you, Henry? This isn't you."

"It's that *thing* in the sky. I'm freaking out!"

"It's more than that."

"No, you don't understand. I *brought* it here."

"You're drunk, Henry. You did not *will* Inanis to just show up in the sky."

Henry shakes his head. "Yes, I did. In the marrow of my bones, I know I brought it here."

Henry looks out the window, the obelisk obstructing his view. He hastily stands up, his balance loosely supported by the touchpoint of the end table.

"*Ex nihilo nihil in nihilum posse reverti*... It's watching me, you know." His speech is slurred, almost a whisper now. "Change is coming. Transmutation is on the horizon."

"You're scaring me, Henry." My voice softens. "Are you taking your meds?" The last part comes in a whisper like a soul leaving its body.

Henry's eyes darken and narrow as they meet mine. He's hurt by the weight of my accusation, but feelings be damned. I need to know.

"Why do you have to go there?"

"Because you sound crazy! Disconnected from reality."

Henry shakes his head. "I've never felt clearer than I do now. Can't you feel it, Jenna? The thrumming of the universe in your veins? A force so apparent, like breathing electricity in shallow bursts. A swell of understanding you cannot ignore."

"Bullshit. It's her, isn't it? Your therapist?" The words fire off and land, a hot mortar with shrapnel slicing everything in its path.

"What?" How could you even say that?"

"I can hear you, you know, laughing from the other side of the door. I thought telehealth appointments were supposed to help you get over your ..." I trail off, unsure how to complete the thought.

"I can't do this right now; I'm going to bed."

As he stands, I grab his wrist like a lifeline before the flood. It startles me, this desperate need to comprehend the shift inside of him. When did our oneness dissolve and force us into opposite corners of the room?

"Is she your friend now? Or is it something more?"

"It's not that, Jenna."

"Then why won't you let me in?" My throat is hoarse and cotton mouthed, my shirt wet from sweat and tears. "Just let me in, Henry. *Please.*"

Henry looks past me, like making eye contact is too painful. As if I'll see something in him I'm not meant to see. The swell of the rift between us a riptide cutting through the current and suddenly I am the one who is floundering. He peers through the window, his focus solely on Inanis now.

"We are atoms connected to everything in this universe. Our ancestors' stardust formed in nebulous clouds. We are part of something greater than human comprehension." His fingers press against the glass. "I wished for this, Jenna. I wished for the end and now it has come. Inanis is *here*. We're going home. So why won't it take us yet?"

The therapist didn't *know* Henry. Didn't know his sorrow had teeth. The pain that festered within his chest cavity was like hag moths taking residence in heart and lungs, revealing itself with the pace of a slug.

He was so focused on the headlines. On the black obelisk outside. As if it had come for him, personally, like it knew the secrets he carried with him.

Henry always did put up a good front. It was his calm demeanor that drew me to him in the first place, that cool headedness amid chaos. But it's easy to be fooled by the tree, strong and stoic, in rising waters when you can't see the intensity of the surge leveraging its roots.

I don't blame the therapist for Henry's suicide. People can only do so much with the tools they are given and the evidence they are presented with. I can even admit to my jealousy, then. I know the therapist was just doing their job. That doesn't mean I'm not angry.

Anger kept me from checking the chamber of the gun. Anger kept me from burying Henry's body. Anger opened my eyes every morning to Henry's corpse rotting in the yard, making sure he was truly gone. I ran blindly through the fog of unbearable loneliness as love died in a vacuum only to chase a man who was already dead long before he pulled the trigger.

It occurs to me that there might not be anything, or anyone, waiting for me at the end of the road. That all this running would once again be in vain toward something I'm not even sure is real. How can I keep fighting to hold onto a man when I barely grasped him in the first place?

The tremor under my feet tells me otherwise.

Empty. Hollow. Tears stream down my cheeks. Bodies and debris sluice their way in and through the veil of darkness like Charon's boat gliding along the River Styx; a steady current that, when looked at from below, could either bottleneck or swallow the world whole.

Maybe it should.

Brilliant and blinding, the opening of Inanis's hollow center absorbs light along with everything floating within it. I run until the ground below me shifts, then separates, destabilizing my footing. Instinct reels my body backward away from the edge of a crumbling overpass. Like the boom of a bass drum and the crashing of symbols, an accompaniment of concrete and rebar unmarry as they ascend toward the heavens. I crouch, run my hands through my hair, and let strands tangle and break under my touch as my mouth turns host to a composer crafting a peon of rage and misery.

Inanis's corona undulates and flares. It shifts its gaze and turns toward me, the only thing in this world that has not yielded to its untenable pull. This is it, the beginning of our exposition. The final sheet of music whose lines are wrought with blood, mud, and tears. Only one of us will prevail in this apocalyptic and mad fugue.

"What do you want from me?!" I shriek, ragged and breathless. "What more could you want that you already haven't taken?"

What more do I want from you? What more could I want that I've yet to take?

The words echo in my mind as Inanis makes itself known to me. I dig in my feet, not willing to accept defeat just yet. I am a cannonball and Inanis is the sea, and though I may lose myself in its depths and sink, I intend to crash through its veil of obscurity. The quest for truth deserves a chance of confrontation, no matter the cost. With nothing more to lose, I stand in the density of my resolve.

I'm so tired. Tired of being angry. Tired of this danse macabre with the other side of existence. A game of chess turned never ending stalemate. This is the precipice to nothing and everything, a final standoff where one must yield to the other. But I do not know how to surrender.

I do not know how to surrender.

Inanis augments my own perception of this reality, and we find ourselves in counterpoint. Our truths exposed. It's reproduction of my own thoughts and feelings tonal in answer.

The universe yawns. The chasm sighs its death rattle, and the inky blackness of space envelops everything. My heart drops as my body freefalls until, finally, I am suspended in an inversion of time. The monotonous clicking returns and plucks away at invisible paddle keys stringing together a secret message I do not understand.

Dark whispers caress my cheeks. Shadowy tendrils traverse my neck, arms, and hands gently nudging my fingers in invitation to open unto Inanis. Crow's feet lines, beaming smiles, coastal sunsets and Wicklow from behind, the light from my phone winks into oblivion, erasing the last vestiture of my memories.

All except one.

I tighten my grip around the stone. Inanis wraps itself around my hand in kind.

"You can't have it," I whisper through muffled sobs.

You can't have it.

Inanis loosens its grip, only slightly, in response. Watching me. Waiting for me to let go. But if I let go, if I relinquish the one thing that anchors me to this plane, then what's left?

What's left?

What comes next in this stretto of plasma waves and uncertainty?

Uncertainty.

When he was alive, Henry would go on about The Bombe, how Alan Turning and Gordon Welchman developed this incredible machine to break the German Enigma code. He was fascinated with the cryptic languages woven into the very fabric of their world like invisible strands that, once tugged, unspooled a thread of unimaginable terrors and truths. That at the end of the day everything could be broken down into *zeroes and ones* reducing every question in the known universe to a set of numbers.

We are part of something greater than human comprehension.

I hated Henry's explanation then, when I couldn't see past my own needs and self-interest. When I didn't understand that there was something beyond our lived experiences in these bodies. The conservation of mass and energy constant, neither created nor destroyed.

Ex nihilo nihil in nihilum posse reverti.

I unfurl my fingers and let the stone slip away.

My breath hitches in my chest. I really wish I could have had that cigarette today.

"Goodbye, Henry."

Goodbye.

The universe collapses. Particles of matter stretch and compress into a disk that spins, rolls, and increases in axial precession at unfathomable speed. Dark matter destroys the laws of physics, and my conscience witnesses the binary Henry sensed thrumming beneath all of existence.

Ribbons of light emerge from the concave of the framework of the universe. Particle points that transform and transport me to that place where everything fades away into sweet nothing, that inexplicable space between life and death, heaven and hell. A final rotation and snap—the plane flattens then expands.

Henry is there, waiting for me.

I reach for his hand, my lips trembling. Maybe none of this is real. Theoretical and imagined, or a projection from Inanis itself. A dream within a simulation of human experience as a means to process deconstruction of our molecular forms. And if this is a dream, then I will let myself surrender to the folly of its magic because Henry's skin is warm against my own. We are together in this ephemeral somewhere at the convergence of the beyond.

Whatever it is, I don't care. It doesn't matter.

It doesn't matter.

Henry holds my hand and smiles. There are no words, for none need to be said. Like the velvet blanket of midnight, or the closing lilt of dust laden blinds after a long day, we spirit away into the event horizon.

I Knew You Were Trouble

By Chris Panatier

The old lady ran through her yard threatening to call the cops. Syd and her gang of older girls sprang up from the melee and bolted. Laura peeled herself off the sidewalk.

"Are you alright dear?" the woman called from her chain-link fence.

Laura stood, tasting blood on her teeth. "I'm okay," she said, collecting the lunchbox that triggered the fight in the first place.

"Come inside, let me get you some ice. We'll call the cops together. Those girls need to be in shackles!"

Laura knew such a thing would only guarantee future beatings. "No, thank you. My house is just a few blocks away." A few blocks being twenty-three blocks.

"At least come inside and let's call your parents."

"They're at work. I just need to get home."

In case Syd and her crew decided to attack again.

"You hold right there for just one second." The lady shuffled quickly into her house and returned a moment later. "Here." She smiled kindly and leaned over the chain-link with a can of Coke. "You can use it to keep the swelling down and then drink it for a pick-me-up. I have three or four per day. It's how I keep a pep in my step!"

Laura accepted the soda. "Thank you." She made a show of holding it against her eyebrow and grinned for the old lady's benefit.

"That's good. You be safe, dear. And stay away from those older girls. They're a pack of hyenas, them. They wait for you, you know, just down by the corner. Maybe choose a different route home from school tomorrow."

Laura said she would without explaining that her route changes had only intensified the hyenas' hunting drive.

She made her way down the crooked walk, cracking the Coke. Her mom said there were twelve tablespoons of sugar in a Coke. She drank until it burned and the sugar rush was like dropping from the top of a roller coaster. Sugar was badass.

She crossed diagonally through the park and alongside an embankment where older kids lit fires and did marijuana. Voices rang up from below, no doubt some of the ones who had beat her up. She slank into the bushes and gazed down to where a creek slithered between the trees. Syd and her gang were on the rocky bank, laughing and joking and probably doing illegal stuff. Laura couldn't understand the words, but she was sure they were reenacting the attack. One of the girls hobbled about in a mime of the old lady who had run them off.

Laura skittered away before they could see her, shooting through the square tunnel that ran beneath the road, up to the train tracks, and finally across into her neighborhood.

Everyday Syd and her friends found a reason to pick on her. She was small. She wore mismatched knee socks. Her mom insisted on cutting her hair and so her bangs were never level. And then, of course, there was her stupid lunchbox. She held it out in front of her. Taylor's eyes and red lipstick were as bright as they'd been when she'd received it for Christmas at eight-years old. It was her favorite possession.

But maybe the hyenas were right. Maybe seventh graders shouldn't be carrying plastic lunchboxes around. Maybe Taylor Swift was for kids. There weren't any other girls in her class who still used a lunchbox. Some of the boys did, but boys were intellectually stunted. She hated to think what she once treasured most in the world had become ass-kicking bait.

Her eyes welled with tears. "Stupid."

Making her way past the self-service carwash, she shoved the lunchbox into the mouth of a trashcan and punched it until it disappeared. Her knuckles were raw, but that isn't why she cried the rest of the way home. Getting rid of the lunchbox felt like she'd thrown part of herself away. She told herself that it was all part of growing up, that at some point you have to stop being a kid. She went to her room and dove onto her bed, where eleven eras of Swift gazed down from the postered walls as she wept into her *Fearless* album sheets.

At dinner, her parents asked about her bloody lip.

"Got hit during kickball."

"That's from a kickball?" said her dad. "I find that–"

Laura's mom gave a quick head shake and her dad went quiet.

"I, uh, I also lost my lunchbox today."

"Also because of kickball?" her dad said with heavy doubt in his voice.

Her mother laid a hand over her husband's wrist. "I'm sure Laura knows we're here if there's anything she wants to involve us in. Right Laura?"

She nodded.

"I'll get you another lunchbox."

"That's okay. I'll just use some of Dad's paper sacks."

And they left it at that.

The next day, Laura packed a bag lunch, strapped on her backpack and headed out.

Breath quivered from between her lips as she straddled the sidewalk. The journey to school was no less perilous than coming home. The first few blocks were usually safe, but once she crossed the train tracks, she'd be exposed. The crossing was a bottleneck, choked on both sides by an old barbed-wire fence and tangles of brush. The other side felt like an untamed wilderness with beasts hiding in the shadows waiting to pounce. If the hyenas meant to come for her that morning, that was where they'd be waiting.

Someone called her name as she passed the carwash, coiling the muscles of her neck and shoulders. She gripped her lunch bag to her chest and looked around. Had Syd and her crew come to her side of the tracks to finish what they'd started before another old lady could chase them away?

The voice came again, thin and grainy, like a cat with bronchitis. "Lauuuuuraaaaaa."

She hurried down the walk, her spine crackling with anxiety.

"Hey! Stop!"

She froze, the muscles in her back cinching tight like shoelaces.

"Yeah you!"

She didn't recognize the voice, but it didn't sound hostile. In fact, it was kind of ... upbeat? Laura scanned the carwash and the adjoining gas station, then across the street to the drycleaner-slash-donut shop.

"Not over there! Over here!"

She spun around, her eyes darting to the trashcan.

"That's right, kid. Come here."

Laura struggled to comprehend what she was dealing with.

"I'm in the garbage, kid."

She baby-stepped closer until she could see into the trashcan. Nothing. Just garbage.

"My question for you, kid, is who throws away a perfectly good lunchbox? So what if they make fun of you? That's their problem. Insecure little skanks. They're missing something in their own lives, so they tear other people down. It's a tale as old as my underpants."

Laura inched closer, searching for whoever was hiding in the trash. "Who—who's in there? Is that you, Katie?" Laura's friend Katie played pranks, but she lived on the other side of town and never mentioned her underpants.

"No Katie in here, Laura. Just me, Bad Truboblix. But you can call me Trouble."

"What are you doing in the trash can?"

"I eat garbage."

"Seriously. Who's in there?"

"Seriously, I like the taste. Don't judge me."

"I'm not judg-"

"Let's talk about this lunchbox, Laura. You can't let them control you. One day it's a lunchbox and the next it's how you dress, then how you act and before you know it, you've become just like them! Sold out to be something you're not. Got me?"

"I ... think so."

"When you give in to what bullies want, you give part of yourself away. Give in, give up. You want to be just like Syd and her poxy gang of lip gloss spangled turds? Is that what you want?"

"How do you know about Syd–"

"Is that what you want?" the voice hissed.

"No!"

"Then take this back!"

The lunchbox shot out of the trashcan and slapped the sidewalk with a rattling clang.

Laura picked it up, more relieved to be reunited than she'd anticipated. She leaned into the trash. "Truboblix? Trouble?"

No answer.

"Are you there?"

Silence.

Laura pushed down on the trash, through snack wrappers and crumpled beer cans until she was convinced nobody was there. Maybe someone had her lunchbox on a string, though there were no strings on it now. The latch was bent, making it impossible to open. She shook it next to her ear, the remnants of yesterday's lunch thumping the walls like shoes in a clothes dryer.

She didn't know what to make of the encounter. There were lots of things that happened in the world she didn't understand. Being a kid was like waiting for a play to start. At some point she would be an adult. The curtain would open and things would make sense. She shoved the lunchbox into her backpack and headed toward school, letting her happiness at being reunited with her favorite possession overshadow any lingering confusion.

Laura slowed as the train crossing approached, cautiously inspecting the angles beyond the trees as far as her eyes would allow. No people, at least that she could see.

Her spine tingled as she slipped safely through, then ran alongside the tracks and skipped onto the bicycle path. It veered across the edge of an old dairy plant, then hemmed Chalmers Graveyard before dipping into the square tunnel under the road. Good progress. There was just the tunnel, then the creek path, the trail through Jo Allen Park and she'd be in the clear.

It wasn't until she rounded the corner that she saw Syd Ryner. The head hyena leaned cooly against the concrete wall with a large Frappuccino in one hand and her phone in the other. Syd was only a year older, but she had giant boobs and dressed like a high school junior. Laura skipped to a stop and began running through escape options.

"What's the matter, Cheez-It? You look like you're trying to hold in a fart."

The Cheez-It nickname was because of a fifth grade field trip when she'd overdone the crackers and threw up in the Doctor Fish display at the city aquarium. It was gonna stick forever.

Syd waved an easy hand. "Come on through. I won't hurtcha." She waved her phone at her head. "Not in a fighting mood. Don't want to mess up my hair."

Laura glanced back to where the path forked for the long way around. "I think I'll go this way."

"Nah. That path goes through the golf course. You'll be late for school." Syd resumed scrolling on her phone.

Laura turned to leave, and Syd made a *tsking* sound. Then Laura saw why. Four more girls rounded the corner of the tunnel.

"Told you to come on through, Cheez-It. I'm not throwing hands today. Free pass. Promise."

Laura's cheeks drained cold as the girls crowded in. Head down, she marched into the square mouth of the tunnel, right past Syd, who made no move except to offer an easy smile. Laura considered Syd's expression as she passed, thinking it almost friendly. No one followed. She was free.

The impact on the crown of her head was disorienting at first. The object had been heavy enough to knock her head downward but had also given like a water balloon. Only it wasn't water that drenched her back and cascaded down her face. The hyenas cackled as she turned slowly around, squeegeeing the Frappuccino from her eyes.

Syd shrugged. "No hands."

"There's a straw stuck in your hair," laughed Lacy Falcone, squinting through a canary shade of yellow eyeshadow.

Hot rage filled Laura's chest, but she turned away, stopping only when she heard the voice from earlier coming from her backpack.

You gotta fight back, kid.

Trouble.

"I can't," she whispered.

Then you'll become a shell of yourself, said the goblin. *Or worse, become like them.*

Andrea and Amy Cross pressed close. They wore matching red leggings even though they weren't twins but always lied and say they were. They even managed to get held back in school together. "Who are you talking to?" their voices were like a pair of out of tune door ringers.

"No one," said Laura.

"What's the matter with your ears, anyway?" said Andrea.

Laura reached up reflexively. The cartilage of her ears had grown thin and leathery.

I told you.

Laura shifted her feet to run.

"No, no, no you don't," said Lacy, seizing Laura's backpack. "Syd may have said she wouldn't throw hands, but me? I had sugar cereal this morning and I'm all full of energy." She popped her fist against her palm.

You gotta show them that they can't do this to you!

"There's no way!" cried Laura.

There's always goblin mode!

"Huh?"

"She's talking to herself," said Amy. "Hey Cheez-It, are you a 'tard or something?"

Punch the little poophole in the face, or this will never stop.

Laura had never fought back in her life. These girls were thirteen and fourteen. Big and strong and not afraid of pain since they'd already gotten their periods. In fact, Laura felt like she was shrinking. Andrea pulled a long, pink string of gum from between her teeth and tossed it, hitting Laura across the face. "No little old ladies to save you this time."

Do something or I will.

Laura was paralyzed.

Three, two, one, here I come!

Her backpack shifted and her lunchbox ejected like bread from a toaster, landing on the concrete. Taylor Swift's brilliant visage sang dreamily up from the lid.

The latches popped and the lid sprang open with a puff of stinking, purple gas.

Something hunched and sinuous emerged. Black, pipe-cleaner arms stretched wide, planting skeletal hands to the ground. The body lifted out from within, a rounded back covered in thick horsefly hairs. Stunted legs dangled from the torso.

The creature dropped to the ground on tiny feet laced in dirty, toe-curled slippers. Batlike ears unfurled from either side of a squat, oblong head. Yellow eyes peeled open as if from an ancient hibernation.

"What the fuck is that?" said Syd, plastering herself to the wall of the tunnel.

"Bad Truboblix!" Laura said, fearing what was to come.

The goblin clapped his hands and danced a jig, tipped his tiny purple bowler hat, and spread his arms into genuflection. "Pleased to make your acquaintances. The name is Trouble, trash goblin, Esquire, and I'd like to speak with the manager, please." He smiled wide, revealing purple gums bulging with crooked rows of barbed teeth, and blinked daintily.

"What do you want?" asked Syd, as if she was talking back to her math teacher.

"Week old bean chili fermented in a Styrofoam box," said Trouble. "But I don't see any of that around! I guess your face will have to do!"

The goblin leapt like a cricket, covering twenty feet through the air before slamming into Syd and dragging her to the ground. The hyenas shrieked and scrambled like fleas from the back of a dog dropped in a hot bath.

Next came Syd's muffled cries as the goblin scratched and bit and tore at her flesh.

"Trouble!" shouted Laura, sprinting to the goblin and grabbing its shoulders. He couldn't have weighed more than forty pounds but was strong and wiry like a chimpanzee. Try as she might, Laura couldn't get him away, and Syd wasn't going to last much longer. Without thinking, Laura snatched the little bowler hat from the back of his head.

The goblin dismounted Syd leaving her sprawled in a puddle of blood with her face torn to shreds. "That's my hat, kid."

"Look what you did to Syd!"

Trouble shifted his angular hips and licked the blood from his fingers as he admired his work. "That's how people look after goblin mode."

"She's really hurt! We have to call the police!"

Laura didn't have a phone, but Syd did. She plucked it off the concrete.

"No!" shouted Trouble, swatting it out of her hand. "She'll live. Her face will just look ... different. *Aaaaaand* she won't bother you anymore, will she?"

"She's missing an eye!"

"Nah, it just looks like that in all the blood." He grabbed the bowler hat and placed it delicately over a tuft of blonde hair atop his head. "Let's get to school before you're late."

"School? We can't go to school. Those other girls will have told everyone what we–what *you*, did."

"Eh-eh, now," said Trouble, ticking his finger. "I was perfectly happy to sit in your lunchbox nibbling on yesterday's sandwich crusts, but you were letting yourself get pushed around. Couldn't let that happen." He cha-cha'd to the lunchbox and stepped inside. "To school, where we will hunt down the remaining aggressors! Don't make me play with your face too, Laura! Speaking of, you might want to get that checked out."

Laura's hands flew to her face and felt the bristled, twisting hairs of her eyebrows. They'd grown bushy and long just like Trouble's.

"What's happening?!"

"You haven't been listening!"

The goblin crunched himself into a stinking little ball and smashed into the lunchbox.

"Close this, will you?"

Laura slammed the lid and latched it, then carried the lunchbox to the far end of the tunnel and launched it into Kendig Creek. She ran back to Syd, who stood holding her face, blood seeping between her fingers.

"You need to go to the doctor."

Syd backed away, eyes wide with fear. "Get the fuck away from me, you little creep."

"But–"

"Away!" she screamed before stumbling off.

Laura watched her go, then considered the bloodstained ground with horror.

Going home wasn't an option, and it wouldn't help anyway. She needed to get to school before the story got out of hand. She tightened the straps of her backpack and ran the rest of the way.

School was normal. Kids laughed at her hair, matted with Frappuccino, but mostly they pointed at her face and giggled. Between first and second periods, she flew to the bathroom and looked in the mirror. Her eyebrows were like a pair of black caterpillars and her ears twisted at the tips like fallen leaves.

She tested a smile, exposing her teeth. "Oh no."

Her gums had pulled away from her teeth, which were now brown at the roots and going crooked. She drew the hoodie of her sweatshirt down to her eyes. The bathroom door opened. She ducked past a pair of girls and rushed to homeroom.

Ms. Holland was writing on the whiteboard when Laura crept in. The fake twins were there, too, sitting to either side of her desk as pallid as a pair of nightcrawlers. Laura oozed quietly into her seat and began mindlessly digging in her bag.

Ms. Holland turned to the class and sighed, but her face lit up when she saw Laura. She went behind her desk for something, then held up a dented and dripping Taylor Swift lunchbox.

"This was right outside the class in the hallway, Laura. Luckily, you're the only girl that still carries one of these, so I knew it was yours. I'm afraid it's seen better days. Try to keep track of your property, 'kay sweetie?"

She set it on the desk.

The twins reacted like it was a bomb. The tinkling of claws against metal came from inside, then Trouble's grimy voice. *I smell the stink of nasty little trollops!* The lunchbox began to shake.

Laura rose from her seat and bellied over it. Amy and Andrea, fully aware of what was inside, shoved out of their desks and scrambled away like a couple of roaches.

"Everyone settle down," said Ms. Holland. "Please return to your seats!"

The lunchbox exploded open, sending Laura over the back of her chair and onto the cold, hard ground.

Bad Truboblix uncurled from within a cloud of putrid stench with a showman's flair. "Ah! What a time to be alive!" He stretched his arms wide and groaned like an old man getting out of bed. "Gotta get back to my yoga."

Ms. Holland made herself a human shield before a scrum of terrified students. The goblin twisted around, until he found Amy and Andrea huddled in each other's arms. "You two the ones been making fun of my client's lunchbox?" He hawked a gelatinous glob of phlegm into his hand

and tossed it, hitting Amy across the face. Andrea's nostrils twitched, then she vomited a rainbow stream of milk and Lucky Charms.

"Don't waste that!" Trouble scrabbled on all fours to the puddle of puke and lapped at it like a dog, snatching Andrea's ankle when she tried to retreat, his jagged claws burrowing into her skin. She wailed and kicked him away.

The goblin sat back onto a crooked stub of tail. "Aw, who's afraid of little old me?"

"Leave them alone."

The goblin's ears perked, and his head twisted around like owl hearing vermin skittering through grass. Narrowing his urine-hued eyes at Laura, he growled, "What did you say to me?"

Her voice shook. She could barely get the air from her lungs to travel across her vocal cords. "I ... said ... uh, leave them alone."

Trouble swiped the books and pens from a nearby desk. "Leave them alone? Oh, no, no, no. A goblin's work is never done. They've got to be taught a lesson. And if you won't do it ..." He dove at Amy's foot and bit through the canvas of her sneaker. She howled and collapsed like she'd stepped in a cartoon snare.

Ms. Holland lunged for the goblin, but he wheeled and popped a boil on his cheek, sending a spray of steaming pus over the teacher's face. The teacher wailed like the Wicked Witch of the West dowsed with water. He cackled and flipped her off as she stumbled blindly into the whiteboard.

"Stop!" cried Laura.

"Stop! Stop!" laughed Trouble. "You belong with me, don't you see? You're becoming a goblin too! And then you won't be a coward anymore!"

"No. You stop. Go away. I mean it!"

The goblin hopped onto a desk and play-acted a sad face. "*You mean it*, do you?"

Laura's heart thrummed in her throat. Her vision seemed to expand and contract. Holding in tears, she nodded.

The goblin drew one of his claws underneath her chin. Black lips pulled up from the tangled briars of his teeth.

"Or what?"

"Or ... or ..."

"*Or... or... I know!*" The goblin gestured with his hands as if rubbing tears away. "Waaaahhhhh!"

Laura lashed out at him.

Truboblix stuttered backward, falling off the desk, a thick, plastic Frappuccino straw sprouting from his right eyeball. He squealed pig-like as green-yellow fluid glugged from the end of the straw.

Laura slapped her hands over her mouth and gasped. She hadn't meant to physically hurt him. It was a split-second reaction. She approached tentatively. "Trouble?"

The goblin plucked the straw and slapped a hand over his eye. "Didn't think you had it in you, TBH."

"But you, what?"

A smile crawled across the goblin's face. "I did what had to be done, kid. Got you to stand up to a bully. Uh, oh no, uhhhggg."

He went limp, arms flopping lifelessly to the floor tile.

"Oh, no!" Laura knelt.

Trouble opened an eye. "JK, not dead yet. Get me to a trash can. It's the only way."

"Really? You're not joking?"

His eye had shriveled into the socket like a raisin. He held up his hands, curling like a dying insect. "All true! Hand to Dog. To the garbage, please!"

Laura picked up the suddenly very helpless goblin and rushed to the bin by Ms. Holland's desk.

"Not in there!" shrieked the teacher.

"You need to calm down," said Laura.

Ms. Holland's open mouth snapped shut.

Laura set Trouble into the bin. "You're too big!"

"Just push. Stomp me down with your feet. I'll be okay. Quick! I've got other children to help."

The way he said *other children* made Laura pause. Together with a flash of something in his eyes, something like youthful innocence, she saw Trouble in a new light. "Other children. You were once a child, weren't you?"

The remaining yellow eye locked with hers. "I became what I thought others wanted me to be. I left myself behind. And this was the result."

"Oh no."

"Oh yes. It's too late for me! But not for you."

Laura ran a finger along her ears. They'd returned to normal.

"Enough!" shouted Trouble. "To the trash!"

Laura did as he said, pushing the goblin into the garbage and then stomping.

"That's it, just like that, aaaaaaahg, I'm melting, melting!"

She stomped and stomped and stomped until trouble was all gone.

Ivy

By L.P. Hernandez

The bones of the house are strong but porous. Little nooks and crannies no mop could ever reach. So, there are rugs here and there. Some new, some pilfered from a seldom seen spare bedroom. They trap the grime left by long dead feet, of wine spilled from a hasty sip. Years of dust, dander, and hair. So many years a single red strand, or even half a dozen of them, could be explained as belonging to the occupants of the past.

The hardwood seems to draw the cold from the belly of the earth. But it is not your living feet that feel it, Richard. It is your hands. Your *hand*. You rub them together, passing the chill from one to the other but the warmth does not transfer. Only the cold.

It is night and I have gathered my strength for this moment. Richard sleeps, facing away from the window. I am green-eyed, fluttering from the same breeze holding owls aloft. I am a snake constricting the bricks of this building. I am wings. My eyes are limitless, though I prefer this view above all others. From the outside. Richard, a mountain range beneath a new comforter. Rebecca, the foothills facing the opposite wall. Beneath his pillow, the hand that never warms. She accepts this bodily quirk, but in the dark hallways of her mind recalls the former warmth of his hands. Both of them. It would have been a joke much earlier in the relationship. How many times had she held that hand? On their wedding day, certainly. How many times would she have not noticed?

From the window I pass undetected, like a moonbeam, into the room. Crescent, not full. Just a whisper of light. I linger around the rug at the foot of the bed, and under it. There are red hairs beneath, in the nooks and crannies. Red hair and hair made red.

What would we have become, Richard, if there ever was a *we*? The woman who angles her body away from you, as if in sleep knows everything she ignores in daylight, is driving you mad. You told me so once, raising your glass to sip and check the time. One eye on the window I just departed. She was in the room with us then, her picture on your nightstand. I always wondered about it, why you would not face it away for the brief moments we shared the air of this hallowed space. To be fair, most breaths were gasps, inhaled with urgency and forced out between the seams of sealed teeth.

I am no ghost, no storybook specter. I am wood, the hidden skeleton of this home, its creaking steps and triple-locked front door. I am the window glass and the shingles. The pipes are my arteries, and the water is my blood now, flowing to faucets, to the spigot outside through the hose to her garden. I am the roses she does not clip. I can inhabit anything. The wine bottles in the basement growing fuzzy with dust, the wedding ring you place on the floating shelf in the bathroom when you shower. A part of me is there always, in that ring, your familiar fingers rubbing my metal skin hoping the friction will warm them.

My favorite place to be is her dreams. So often of you, so often of this home. So often of things she never sees but senses. Rebecca glides into rooms feeling as if each was occupied until the moment she entered to find them empty. As if the displaced air of their departure creates a vacuum drawing her in. I steer her, like blowing a dust bunny, to the bathroom, the vanity and its plush, velvet-cushioned chair. She reaches for a brush, one she lost on the other side of this dream. Together, we brush her hair. Our hands melt into one.

Rebecca hums, eyes closed, the only other sound the static of the bristles breaking through silver-blonde tangles. Eyes open, pinching fingers, she does not liberate the hair from the brush in this dream because it is not the same color as hers. It is red.

Please don't use her things. I had to throw that brush away and pretend the new one was a gift. One hair could end this.

This. Not us.

This is not a dream, really. More a reality he did not expose her to.

I wanted to know what it felt like to be her.

I promised I would never do it again. But I have, so many times, through her.

Rebecca opens her eyes and blinks at the wall. Richard, in portrait form, is at the top of her vision, out of focus. The roots of the dream shrivel, retreating from her awareness before touching that hidden well of understanding. I watch through Richard's eyes as she blinks, adjusts to this environment, familiar but strange in this light. She is more beautiful than me, than I was, even seconds after waking with drool like an inkblot on her pillowcase. I told Richard this, hoping he would dispute it.

She doesn't have this beautiful red hair.

His fingers were sun-warmed snakes on my scalp, and I was made boneless beneath his touch.

From the nightstand portrait of Richard, I swim to the floorboards. This house is old, and the wood, my new bones, is older, and dry here on the third floor. I pull moisture through its roots, past the fuzzy wine bottles in the basement, and everything else forgotten there. I direct it to the bedroom, to the place beneath the rug where the sun-warmed snakes collapsed around my throat and squeezed until the capillaries in my nose burst. The sight of blood angered him. More to clean and more to hide. Not so angry that he stopped. I was grateful as it filled my ears and stopped me from hearing my last breath.

I felt bones I could not have named crack and shift, free floating in my neck, tearing holes through my blood vessels. I felt, through the pain and confusion, the hardness of his wedding ring below my ear.

The moisture I pull through the house revives the blood in the nooks and crannies beneath the rug. There isn't much of it. I have to be deliberate. Rebecca blinks a few times, each longer than the last. Perhaps a full moon would have been better. There is little light and the floorboards are dark. It must catch the moonlight just so.

A footprint appears on the floor, its toes pointed at the bathroom. Rebecca's eyes are half-lidded, but do not close. Her brows furrow. A second footprint appears a step beyond the first. Fabric shifts, pajamas sliding from beneath the sheets. The floorboards thrum as her heels make contact. But she is feather-light, and the thousand shrieks trapped within my wooden skeleton hibernate through her movements. The white tiles of the bathroom floor beckon. She stops, looks over her shoulder, then proceeds, holding her breath as she passes the bloody footprints.

The contrast is greater in the bathroom, so less blood is necessary. Just enough to show the way. Rebecca does not close the door, maybe fearing the click of the latch would wake him. Perhaps a closed door would be more suspicious than an open one. One bloody footprint, in the center of the bathroom and aimed at the walk-in closet, pulls her toward it like water circling a drain.

Richard knew I was not as beautiful as his wife. That I was *not* her was my greatest appeal. That and my hair. She is at the border between the closet and bathroom. Her heart beats so forcefully it interrupts her breaths, as if someone is pounding her spine with the heel of a hand.

Richard's wardrobe is mostly black business suits. No band t-shirts. No football jerseys. Every clothing item serves a purpose. I died in a mint green dress with brown polka dots. It was the dress I wore the night we met. It was the dress I wore when I felt him slipping away from me.

I am wearing it now.

What is left of me.

I pass through the walls to the railing. Fourteen black blazers, so similar even he cannot tell them apart. Fourteen black blazers but only one with a lock of red hair tucked inside an inner pocket. He takes it out sometimes, smells it though the scent is more starch than my shampoo or perfume. His heart beats faster when he does this, like Rebecca's does now as the hanger tilts and the blazer slips free, falling to the floor.

"Hello?" Rebecca whispers.

She places a hand to her belly and swallows.

The machinery of her mind misfires. There is her future with this man, with the still secret cargo protected by her hand. There is the marrow-deep knowing Richard is hiding something. The impression in the velvet of the cushioned chair, of a pair of legs off to the side rather than facing forward. A pair of legs a little fuller than hers. As if someone only sat there to see how it felt. The missing brush and the odd, specific reasoning offered.

You deserve the best.

It sounded like a lie because it was, so inartful in the telling she believed it, because the alternative was her husband was a very, very simple man. And what did that suggest of her?

So many other signs, and now this. The blazer mostly retains its shape on the floor. The muscle beneath her left eye twitches. With her right hand, she rolls her fingers over the fabric of her nightdress. She circled tomorrow's date in her planner. It is an anniversary of theirs. Not wedding, but something important. First *I love you*, maybe.

In the office trash can there are scraps of paper with dozens of boy names. Rebecca knows it's going to be a boy. Among the names, there is no variation of Richard.

Rebecca squats beside the blazer. Her mouth has become a razor slice, and her eyes show white all around the irises. She hums but sustains the note for only a second before gently clearing her throat. She drapes the blazer over a forearm as she stands, looking at the vacant space on the rack. One toe over the precipice. The other foot is firm behind her, the floor beneath it steady.

She smooths the blazer, and I sense the gravity of her preferred fate. Firm. Steady. But the smoothing hand stops near her navel. Her palm presses the flesh there. Not yet firm from expansion but a bit softer in preparation for it. Rebecca blinks a few times, then her hand disappears within the blazer. When she feels it, her eyes go wide again.

The blazer falls to the floor and my hair is black in the darkness of the closet, a comma on her palm.

I arch my back and the wood beneath the bathroom tiles pops. Rebecca spins to confront the sound, expecting Richard and finding only the footprint. Her nostrils flare, the only suggestion of what she feels.

The bloody footprints in the bedroom hide within wooden whorls, no longer wet and catching moonlight. Mt. Richard faces away, only his hand visible in the confusion of the comforter. It crosses the border between their halves of the bed. In sleep he still reaches for her warmth.

Rebecca reaches the top of the stairs on her own intuition, the same that steers her into empty rooms in her dreams. She licks her lips. The house is so quiet. All its sounds come from outside. She takes a step, not knowing I am stiffening the wood beneath her feet. Rebecca is a ghost now. Quiet and haunted by the possibility plucked from Richard's pocket.

I am not a poltergeist. I am this house. Rebecca swims through my hollow places and I make the path easy for her. My hair is hidden in her knot of a hand, the knuckles like barnacles. None of my vitality endures in that memento. I am as connected to it as the knives in the kitchen drawers, as Richard's books and their glossy, unbroken spines.

She stands at the bottom of the stairs and searches the silhouettes of furniture and curtains. All of it so familiar in the day but so different in this moment. Maybe she believes this is a dream. The feeling is the same. Following an essence with the weight of an idea. There is a light above the kitchen sink. She floats in that direction like a moth, passing photos on the wall of herself smiling wider than it seems possible now.

Rebecca hugs her torso beside the kitchen island. Richard has secrets, and so does she. Most are mundane and endearing. She believes he is too good for her, but not in terms of his character. He is too good for her in the same way a Porsche would be too good for her. The house is too good for her. She told her mother she feels like she is living in a museum.

Well, museums are beautiful, aren't they?

Not to live in. To visit, take pictures, and leave. Museums are for displaying the inaccessible, artifacts evolved beyond utility. It is how Rebecca feels about herself. In this house, with its ivy-wrapped stone carapace, she has only ever felt like a guest, a tourist. She is afraid of breaking things, of leaving traces of herself.

But that's not true, is it Rebecca?

Look at the pictures on the wall. Out in the wild. A date in the botanical gardens and your dress rivaling the brightest petals. A pumpkin patch stroll with your autumn-red sweater, your silver-blonde hair molten with sunlight. You brought color into this house.

(so did I)

You brought color into this house but it clashed with the browns, blacks, and whites.

A slab of light flares across the room. The basement you have never visited because Richard said it was dangerous. The stairs needed work. You didn't question the thunder of his boots over those stairs when he disappeared into the darkness to emerge with a dusty bottle of wine. You didn't question the dirt under his fingernails.

"Hello?"

You whisper this through splayed fingers, swallow, and glance behind at the still staircase. He dropped me on those stairs three times. He hissed about it like a surprised viper. Said he should have cut me into pieces first. Would have if not for the blood.

Have you ever seen the basement? The floor of it? Richard said there were rats down there. The house was old, in his family for five generations. There had always been rats. That is true, but they're visitors only, not permanent residents. They follow the food, and it isn't always there.

I flow to where you'll go next, and in a moment you are right where you are supposed to be. Your hand is warm on the doorknob. This must be why Richard reaches for you. There is a lock, *for the rats*, but I've taken care of that.

The hinges groan like something dying, and your face pinches at the sound. Your elbows press against your ribcage squeezing the breath from your lungs. You know it already, Rebecca. In your soul if not your mind.

What is there to fear if not the man whose hand breeches the meridian of your bed to grab your arm and squeeze, trapped in a dream, his teeth like candle flames in the dark? Your knowing is like tar in your spine, dulling your reflexes.

The light is yellow like a December moon. Dust clots the tattered spider silk, turning fallen webs into scraggly beards. It is how you imagined it would be, old and uninviting. With each step, your tar warms, your limbs growing supple, movements effortless. In the ten minutes you have held my hair you have thought of no reason for its existence, for its presence in his pocket.

The first step accepts your weight in silence, as does the second. Your free hand touches the wall for an instant, cool as a snake's belly. The down on your arm rises, quivering golden filaments. You inhale the scent of exposed dirt. Of rat feces. Of me. The hand holding what is left of me above ground rests upon your navel as the effluvium stimulates the acid in your belly. I am so close to what you and Richard created.

He created me too, Rebecca. In a way.

The next step feels as sturdy as the first two. With your mind elsewhere, you do not recognize the wood here is soft and rotten, that there is nothing to grasp as you fall.

The sound of your tibia snapping would have frightened the rats away. But there is nothing left of me to consume, and the rats are elsewhere for now. What is left of me is buried, not deep enough, twenty feet away. You do not know this. Your mouth is a cavern, but there is no breath to power a scream.

Richard wakes with honeyed light spilling over the comforter. His mummy arms, both of them, reach for the place she no longer occupies. Her side of the bed is unmade, which is unusual. If she wakes up before him, she tidies the bed.

She leaves no trace.

"Becca?"

His voice is meant to travel as far as the bathroom. Hers has not made it to the bedroom. With her greatest effort, it died halfway up the stairs. She screamed for Richard. She screamed from pain. She screamed when, attempting to escape, a step buckled and on instinct, she put weight on her broken leg. When the bone ripped through the flesh like a shark fin emerging from the depths.

She screamed when the first rat nipped her calf. They are easy to guide from one end of the property to the other. A scent. A sound. Had I led them by a leash they would have arrived no faster. And Richard slept, reaching for her.

The floorboards creak in their usual places. The bloody footprints are barely noticeable. And he doesn't notice them.

Rebecca's back touches the stone wall. The light bulb flickers because the wiring is as old as the cleft chin in Richard's family line. She is still beautiful, even now. She gags. From pain or from recognizing the rusty smell of her own blood. The stairs beckon on her left. Three are now piles of splinters on the basement floor. Two yellow eyes hover on the border of the intermittent light. She has no weapon, nothing to threaten it with.

Richard stands in the bathroom with his hands on his hips. The bloody footprint on the floor he cannot ignore. In the closet, the blazer is on the floor. He knows which of the fourteen blazers it is. His lips pool on one side of his face as he chews the inside of his cheek. Rebecca knows ... *something*.

Rebecca presses harder into the basement wall, as if hoping to become part of it.

Not yet, Rebecca.

You have to die first.

Richard returns the blazer to its hanger, examines the paint splatter pattern on the ceiling as he strides through the bathroom and back to his side of the bed. He unlocks his phone, opens his contacts, and locates *Jim – Lawyer*.

He takes a single, steadying breath, pops his neck on both sides, then practices smiling. He practices shrugging with one eyebrow arched.

The rat no longer flinches when Rebecca hisses. It nurses from the puddle of blood left by the wound of her ruined leg. Spilled blood was a compromise. There are more coming. Her dry tongue probes the pixelated surface of her lips. She wonders if a person could die from a broken bone. Probably not, but it is not just a broken bone. She cannot feel her leg below the wound, and blood is still flowing out of her.

Richard grips the banister, shifting his weight onto it. The noisy stairs only mouse squeak beneath his bare feet. He no longer calls for her, likely preferring the advantage of surprise. His body reacts before the thought forms in his mind. He flexes his fingers, glances around the room below searching for her, or searching for a weapon. Something blunt.

Will his mind change when he sees her? Sees how close she is to death.

He stands in the foyer, looks left to right, hands back on hips. If Rebecca had the strength to scream now, he would probably hear her. There is no evidence of her presence, though that is typical. Maybe she left. He retrieves his cell phone and hovers his index finger above *Call*.

His countenance shifts, the bunched muscles under his eyes relaxing. His sneer loosens into a smile.

He clears his throat and whispers, "It was from work. Yeah, testing some new dyes and they needed something organic–"

The mask slips. The relaxed muscles bunching like fruit shriveling in the sun.

Richard only ever called it *the office* around me. Always huffed in a dismissive tone. He talked about *Jack* and *Daryl*. He talked about their secretaries and their wives.

Phone momentarily forgotten, he whispers, "It was my mom's. Before she let her hair go gray. Yeah, she ... No. Fuck. She'll ask her about it."

In the basement, Rebecca rouses from a brief slip into unconsciousness. Her back is against the wall, ruined leg extending into darkness and the other bent at the knee. From a dream, she emerges into a nightmare. Her leg is cold, disconnected, like an arm trapped under a pillow during sleep. The light bulb fizzles out, and her memories of even ten minutes ago elude her like a night-colored snake in the garden.

The light hums back to life, and her head is tilted to her left. Three broken stairs and a rectangle of light framing the door above them. Her eyes sink to the wine bottles as the dark reclaims its territory. She remembers the sound of her bone snapping and reaches for her leg. On the floor above, Richard has settled on aggressive defiance. His temples pulse like two mouse hearts. Rebecca's phone is on her nightstand, buzzing.

Her probing hand touches her knee, thankfully intact. Next, it grazes something wet, and twitching. As her phone thrums on the nightstand, the basement light flashes in a strobe pattern, illuminating a small army of rats. There are two in the open fracture, wet like miniature seals. The silhouette of her foot is different. The toes are a mountain range of bone peaks and flesh valleys. The assault is bloodless as no blood is flowing there. Rebecca, two hands resting on her belly, finally screams loud enough to be heard.

Upstairs, Richard's face relaxes again. The future is undecided, best not to commit to a single possibility.

"Rebecca?"

He scrutinizes the doorframe, and I mend the frayed wiring well enough to make the basement light pulse, banishing shadows and answering any question of where the scream originated. He twists the knob with his cold hand and allows gravity and the slight tilt of the house's foundation to do the work of opening the door.

"Rebecca?"

He crosses the threshold. That Rebecca found the hair and is in the basement where I am buried is troubling. That those truths would be happenstance is unlikely.

"Rebecca? What are you doing?"

Richard squints at the smudges of color at the bottom of the stairs. The shadows have reshaped Rebecca into something unrecognizable.

"Who is that? Hello?"

"Hello again," I reply, shaking his hand. He doesn't catch the second word in the greeting, or he dismisses it.

His lips part, but he doesn't speak as he considers offering a false name. Something about me feels familiar, though, trustworthy.

"Richard."

"Penelope."

"That's a beautiful name. Kind of uncommon nowadays."

It is the first and second-to-last time he will use that word to describe anything related to me. Beautiful. He buys a drink and offers it with his left hand, allowing the incandescent glow of the overhead lights to ignite the silver of his wedding band. He smiles, then I do.

"*Well, that's out of the way now,*" *he says.*

He doesn't recognize me, but of course he wouldn't. I didn't look like this the first time.

More is buried in this basement than my body. More secrets. More bodies. Some Richard's doing. Some not.

"I'm pregnant," she sighs, as if directing the comment at the rats gnawing her toes.

"What?" Richard asks. He remembers his phone, turns on the flashlight and holds it up as if at a concert.

His mind must have reconstructed the staircase. Filled in the blank spaces. Though his reflexes were sharper than Rebecca's, it only meant he fell the twelve feet to the basement floor with his arms outstretched. His phone is on the landing.

"Rebecca?"

"Over here," she mumbles.

Rats flee from his plodding steps. No broken bones for Richard.

Rebecca is on the cusp of a dream. I can fully access her there. Something pleasant and much brighter than the murky darkness around her. Not of this house. Not of Richard. A smaller house and a woman she planned to call with good news.

"Rebecca?"

Richard is on his knees, probing. Her blood is cold beneath his fingertips, and that makes it less recognizable, though he has touched it many times before. His heart is beating so hard. I can feel it through his feet.

"What happened? What did you …"

She does not scream when he blindly dips his fingers into the open fracture, and he does not understand what he feels.

"I'll get help," Richard says, eyeing the beacon at the top of the stairs.

The basement light flickers, and they find each other's faces.

"I … would have dyed it," she says, then drifts.

I am not the first woman Richard killed. But I am the first woman he killed more than once. I can flow from soil to stone, from floorboard to faucet. I can flow from a dying hand to a living one.

The beacon is fading, and there are few stairs left to reach it. The wood is just sturdy enough to give him hope, and is a betrayal when the wood buckles and he is on the basement floor again.

Rebecca is still holding a few strands of my hair, but they are not the first she has held. There was the envelope on Richard's desk, unlabeled and conspicuous because of it. Blonde. There was the lock the cleaning lady found dusting the books in the library. Auburn. Richard said she must have brought it into the house.

I flow into Rebecca and inhale her final breaths. Soon I'll sense her elsewhere.

Richard will not flow when he dies. He will ricochet within me until the walls of this house crumble.

"You can't be pregnant," Richard says.

"I am."

"It isn't mine."

"There's been no one else."

"It can't be mine."

His tone changes, no longer an expression of disbelief but a declaration of intentions. I thought he would ask to marry me. I would be the lady of the manor. That strange, beautiful estate he showed me pictures of early in our relationship. What I would do with that garden.

"I'll be back," he says, then leaves the kitchen for his bedroom and closes the door behind. The apartment is small, but he is one of only a few students not living in the dorms. Despite what he might believe, it was not his wealth that attracted me to him, but the way it loosened the sinews in his body. Life would work out for Richard, because it always had. His grades did not matter. His future and inheritance were assured.

The bedroom door cracks open half an hour later. Holding onto hope is like trying to keep a raw egg from slipping between my fingers.

"Okay, Dad," Richard says.

He bypasses the kitchen, not making eye contact, and locks the front door.

"I figured it out, Jenny," he says, back against the door. He inhales through his nose and breathes out through his mouth.

"Figured what out?"

Richard has walked the length of the basement, most of it, more than one hundred times by nightfall. Rats with swollen bellies follow the sound of his movements. A few of them dined on the good news Rebecca was going to share with her mother that day.

Halfway through his third bottle of wine, on his return journey from the absolute darkness of the far end of the basement, he vomits and falls to his knees.

Rebecca is gone. She is now the smoke trailing from the wick of a snuffed candle. I can feel her brushing the grooves of the brickwork. She is exploring, and soon she will find what she pretended not to know was buried beneath the house. A tidal rush of rats scurry past Richard's bent form and he shrieks, pulling his arms close to his body.

I can flow anywhere. I took my time getting to you, Richard. From soil to stone, from stone to a body cold with death. There is enough left for my need.

Richard hides beneath clasped and tented hands. He squeezes his eyes shut, but he hears Rebecca stand, the wet shifting of blood and exposed muscle, bile sloshing around a tattered belly. The rats did not make it to her face, or her neck. She is still beautiful, and her voice is intact when I speak. He kisses the dirt, his body trembling like the ivy leaves constricting the old stones of this house turned mausoleum.

"Hello again."

Picture to Burn

By Gemma Amor

When Anna walked into the bar, every head turned. Not because of the way she was dressed or held herself, but because of the expression she wore on her face. It was one of pure, unadulterated hatred. The blankest, coldest, most resolute expression any of the patrons of the Salty's Bar had ever seen or would ever see again.

She marched across the sticky faux wood floor stained with tomato sauce splashes and week-old beer and fryer fat, each blob and splat preserved forever under a patina of dirty mop water that gave the bar its signature sour, salty smell. A group of men gathered around the pool table at the far end watched her coming, marking her arrival with smirks and whistles, wiggling cocktail sticks poking out between tongue and teeth. They collectively hitched up their belts the closer she got, leaning on the ends of pool cues with raised eyebrows as her boot-clad feet stomped closer.

"Your girlfriend is here, Garrett," one of the men said, unnecessarily.

Garret folded his arms, leaned back, one boot up against the wall behind him, a bottle hanging loosely down by his side, neck inserted between the index and ring finger like he was smoking a cigar.

"Ex," he said. "And I'm not blind."

"Maybe she's after royalties," another man sniggered.

Garrett nodded. He knew why Anna was here. She held the reasons in her left hand. He thought, as she marched towards him, that if she had half as much fire in her when they were together, he might have stayed interested a little longer. As it was, their relationship had been all in for about six months, give or take. Hot and heavy at first, it didn't take long for her to get insecure, needy, to hang around him like a lame fucking puppy to the point he got what he always got. *Irritated.* Unable to take a hint, her clinging hands became claws, as if she was drowning. That always ended the same way for him. Staying out later and later, in this bar, with these people, until the inevitable happened: another Anna, across the pool table, after closing. He'd walked through the front door later reeking of beer and perfume and something muskier, more pungent, something downright dirty. Anna had stayed up waiting for him. One look at Garrett's face and she knew the score.

This time, however, the puppy didn't go down without a fight. She left his place without a word, dumped him before he had a chance to do it first. This struck Garrett as unreasonable. Uppity. Uncivil. Unfair. He couldn't be blamed for his behavior, not when she smothered him so much he felt he had to run away. Then she blocked him everywhere before he had a chance to explain himself.

I just don't see why you're upset, Anna. I never said we were exclusive, I can have as many women friends as I like. I don't like clingy, I like secure, and you ain't that … if anything, this is your fault. You pushed me to it. I got needs, Anna, okay? I got needs.

None of his usual excuses got a chance to land this time around. Anna erased him from her life overnight, on every single social media platform, every number, every app. He went to her apartment but she refused to answer the door and changed the locks the next day. She stopped going to her usual gym, abandoned the bars she used to drink at, including Salty's. She went ghost mode, until she didn't.

Until she told everyone she could that he had a small dick. He heard about it later. She turned up at a party, a mutual friend of a mutual friend, and had a good old time telling everyone and their dog about what an unsatisfactory lover he was, laughing and drawing little sketches of his appendage on beer mats and laughing some more.

That's when Garrett lost his temper.

That's why he did what he did, and why she was here, now, after giving him the silent treatment for so long. Did she think she could humiliate him without consequence?

Think again, whore.

Brave of her to come alone, he thought, as she walked right up to him and stopped. She looked prettier than he remembered: hair long, thick, smooth, skin clear, eyes wide and filled with a strange kind of light. It was like the breakup suited her. Garrett didn't like that, not one bit.

Something ugly stirred in his guts. His grip on his beer bottle tightened.

Uppity bitch.

"Hi Garrett," Anna said, as calm as if she didn't know he could knock her every which way but Tuesday, as if she weren't facing six other men who could do the same.

Garret leaned against the wall, his pose a reminder of how little he cared about her appearance. Secretly, it bothered him that she looked so good. It bothered him that she cut him out of her life so easily. It bothered him that she knew what he had done.

He let none of this show on his face.

Anna held up a piece of paper. A printout, unfolded. On it, Garrett recognized a picture, screenshotted from a site he knew very, very well indeed. Graphic, blurry, harsh lighting from a phone flash. They were both in it, doing what people do when they are drunk and hot and horny. She was legs akimbo; he was making direct eye contact with the camera. He was proud of himself, and it showed. Anna was less enthusiastic, more submissive, just the way he liked his women to look during the act. She was trying to hide her face from the camera with one raised arm but didn't quite manage it quick enough. The distinctive birthmark on her left cheek was clearly visible through the blur of her fingers.

Garrett smirked, mimicking the expression in the photograph, which was one of his favorites.

"You're a piece of maggoty shit, Garrett," Anna said, furiously. "You posted these to that website knowing what it would fucking do to me."

Garrett's smirk widened into a full blown, shit-eating grin. "I don't know what you mean, princess. I've never seen that before."

His friends chuckled, shifting from foot to foot in anticipation of what was about to be a very public argument.

Anna's eyes blazed. Garrett could have sworn the temperature in the bar raised by a degree or two. A bead of sweat trickled between his eyebrows, ran down the side of his nose. He ignored it.

"Revenge porn, Garrett. Pretty fucking low, even for a piece of shit like you. Do you know what happened once these went live? Once you shared it around with all your stupid, dull fucking friends?"

Garrett's eyes narrowed. Where did this newfound courage come from? Meek and timid throughout their short relationship, the Anna he remembered would never have the balls to stand up in front of him like this, chastising him before his brothers as if they weren't even there. Her back was straight, her posture confrontational. She wasn't scared of him, he realized, and that made him feel all sorts of ugly.

The temperature in the bar rose another notch. The fidgeting around him intensified. The boys were raring to go, he could smell fight on them. One brother put two fingers up, wiggling them in a lewd gesture that was part come-here, part finger-fuck. Anna was flirting with trouble, real trouble, with only a couple of feet between her and a very, very nasty end to her ill-advised trip to Salty's.

Garrett shrugged. Another trickle of sweat ran down his back, right between his shoulder blades. He could smell himself.

"And?" he said, nonchalance personified, or so he hoped.

She took another step forward. Garrett frowned. His skin prickled. Something about Anna's presence made him suddenly uneasy, although he couldn't say why. There was a palpable energy around her that didn't feel right. Hard to describe, but she gave off heat, somehow. Like she was a crackling forest fire in the distance. Her hair seemed to be full of static, climbing away from her body and slowly, strand by strand, floating up into the air around her head. Nobody else apparently noticed this but him.

Was she on something? She looked wired as fuck.

"I lost my fucking job at the school," Anna said then, eyes huge. Her pupils caught all the light in the bar and threw it back out like she was glowing.

"I worked for years to get that job, and you fucked my life with one click of a mouse," she went on, voice cracking. "And you know what you did. You fucking know. It wasn't enough to upload those photos, those videos you took without my consent. You sent that link to my whole class too, didn't you? God fucking knows how you got ahold of my email lists, but you fucking did. My whole class has seen me like this, and I cannot hold my head up anywhere in this town anymore. Everyone has seen these photos, Garrett. My mom, my dad, my cousins, my friends, my pupils, the other teachers at the school I no longer work at. Even the fucking staff in the grocery store. Not to mention these fuckers, who I am sure had a great time jerking off to us."

Anna's hair continued to climb up around her head. It looked eerie, unnatural. The other men behind Garrett began to pay attention, at last.

"What's going on with her eyes?" one of them muttered, frowning. "She got contacts in or something?"

Garrett pushed himself away from the wall, stretching himself up to his full height to remind his ex of who was boss, here, who had the physical advantage, if not the moral high ground.

"I lost my job," she continued, undeterred. "I couldn't pay my mortgage, so I lost my apartment, and my parents can't look me in the face anymore. You happy, Garrett? All of this, because I told everyone you had a tiny dick?"

Garrett examined the fingernails on his left hand, taking his time before he answered.

"I mean," he said, slowly, not feeling anywhere near as unbothered as he tried to sound. "Yeah. And?"

Anna narrowed her eyes, glowing red, not even a trick of the light, just *glowing* with a malevolent, raw light that almost hurt to see, and licked her lips.

"And, this," she said.

She pulled out a Zippo lighter with a scratched, silver casing and a little gold emblem on the side. She thumbed the lid open. Snapped her fingers next to the lighter wheel.

A spark turned into a flame. The flame flickered, tonguing the explicit printout photo, which browned on contact, then caught and began to burn. Orange flames licked the paper greedily, climbing higher and higher.

Anna did not seem to worry about the fire burning her fingers. She maintained intense eye contact with Garett, who was now more confused than ever.

"Crazy bitch," one of the men guffawed from behind the pool table, which he positioned between himself and the girl with the burning picture, just in case. Nobody echoed him. There was a tension in the bar that was tangible, nasty, like the whole place was dry tinder waiting to go up, not just the printout in the girl's delicate grip.

Garret squirmed, his pants feeling suddenly too tight, the fabric of his shirt catching and snagging against his skin. His feet shifted uncomfortably, they were hot in his boots. He stamped them on the floor several times, hard, as if he had pins and needles. It didn't help. The heat continued to rise around him, and his toes were suddenly consumed by a red, red pain, as if…

"Garrett, your fucking feet, man! Lookit your feet!"

Frowning, Garrett did as instructed. His soles were smoking.

What the fuck?

There wasn't time to think anything more than that. Before he could take another step back, both feet burst into flames.

Garrett screamed. His friends fell to the sides of the bar. The smoke intensified. The smell of singed socks, burning leather, and, finally, searing flesh filled the air. Someone snatched up a pitcher of beer, threw it at him. The beer sizzled as it hit but had little effect.

Garrett was burning, from the toes up.

The pain was the worst thing he'd ever felt in his life.

Anna's eyes glowered, redder than ever. Her hair stood fully on end so that it made a distinct, odd, blonde crown around her skull. She did not smile. She remained deadly serious as the picture, and the man, continued to blaze.

Garrett, unable to move from shock, from pain, from confusion, looked at his feet again. Flames licked up from the tops of his boots and started working up his jeans towards his knees. He was burning, he realized, in the same direction as the picture Anna was holding: from bottom to top.

"Anna," he yelled, eyes wide in horror. "Anna, what are you doing?!"

Someone else started beating at him with their leather jacket, trying to smother the flames as they raged higher and hungrier up Garrett's body. All he could do was stand there, helpless with agony. All efforts to smother the fire were futile: water, beer, smothering, none of it worked. No sooner had one flame been put out, than another leaped up to take its place.

"Stop it, you crazy bitch!" A voice shouted, from behind the smoke quickly filling up the bar. "You're killing him!"

Anna shrugged. "And?" she said. The picture held before her was almost done. Garrett was not. He saw, through tears, the paper shrivel to ash, which dropped to the floor.

Anna dusted her fingers thoughtfully.

And in an instant, the flames consuming Garrett's clothes, petered out.

He sank to the floor, sobbing, holding his charred arms out in front of him, the brown, crispy flesh exposed now his shirt had burned away. He was half-naked, he realized. His pants and underwear, and the lower half of his shirt and sleeves had fully melted away, like his skin.

Except…

As he watched, he saw the impossible: skin, re-saturating, the burned color receding, the usual soft pink growing back, like a stain spreading across silk sheets. The massive burns on his feet, ankles, thighs, and forearms healed themselves as rapidly and aggressively as the fire which had consumed him only moments before.

He looked up at Anna, shaking from trauma as his body knitted itself back together and grew a fresh new layer of unblemished skin, moles and freckles and hair right back as it had been before.

Was he hallucinating? Was he drugged? What the fuck was happening?

"You dumb bitch!"

Patrons scrambled for exits, for phones to call 911, for water, for blankets, for fire extinguishers in case the flames came back. Garett knew he should keep his mouth shut, but he could not help himself. Fear induced rage flooded him from head to toe, an agonizing onslaught of sensation that drove him wild, and he stood up as best he could on his blackened, crabbed, ravaged feet, spitting and snarling at his ex-girlfriend as his skin continued to regrow. The rebirth, he found, was almost more painful than the burning.

Almost.

"Pictures on the internet live forever, don't you know that?" Garett continued, defiant, emboldened by his healing. His voice was raw, smoke-choked, as if he had been strangled. He swayed like a tree about to go down but managed to hold himself upright so he could stare his ex down, like she deserved. "Even if you get them taken down, they'll survive. Digital footprints last a long, long time, Anna. Your fucking legs will be open to anyone who wants to see what you got between them, forever. Ain't no wiping that shit away once it's out there."

Anna stared at him with her ember-bright eyes and nodded, just once, as if deciding something.

Then, she pulled another printout from her pocket. Unfolded it. In this picture, a different screengrab from the same website, the same horrible logo at the top, the same vitriolic comments below printed out in minute commentary, she was tied up. Her eyes were half-closed, her clothing absent. She was trying to smile for him, but it was not a smile of enjoyment. It was a smile of endurance. She had bruises on her arms and legs. The same bright flash bleached her skin, washed out her dignity.

"Exactly," she said, only this was the real-life version of her, not the version exposed for a world of strangers to see. "Exactly."

Too late. Garrett realized that the decision she had made was whether or not he had learned his lesson.

Clearly, she had decided not.

"No!" he wailed, but it was no use.

The lighter clicked. Anna lit the second printout on fire. As the paper took and flickering orange flames turned her shame and humiliation brown, indistinguishable, Garrett let fly a horrible, ear-splitting scream, slapping at himself with his fingers baby-soft, newborn tender. Half his friends had abandoned him, he saw, having run out the back and into the night, pool cues abandoned on the table and floor. A bartender pulled the pin out of a fire extinguisher and sprayed white, sticky foam all over him in a desperate attempt to put him out. The flames, brighter and fiercer than ever, consumed the foam, ignoring the rules of physics and combustion and evaporating the white stuff into oblivion. Another patron ran at Anna brandishing one of the discarded pool cues, intent on knocking her out, to end the torture, but she intercepted him with a brilliant, glowing-red glance. The man, a total stranger to Garrett, dropped his pool cue, turned tail and ran.

Garrett, meanwhile, was up to his neck in fire. He could smell himself cooking, feel his extremities crisping up, going hard, crumbling, dropping to the floor. He held the stumps of his arms up, screeching at the sight of bones protruding from each wrist. His feet were gone too. He could feel his hair was on fire, his eyelashes, his beard. The stench of himself in his nostrils was overwhelming. He gagged, found his throat filled with thick, acrid smoke.

"Help ... me!" He held one charred stump out, pleading. Anna remained unmoved, unmoving, as the second picture slowly disappeared in her grip.

Garrett had no choice but to wait as that printout crumbled to ash. When it did, he collapsed to the ground and stayed there, fully naked, skin crisped from head to toe, shuddering and convulsing on the melted linoleum as his ravaged form began to do what it did last time: heal, at a supernatural rate. Blisters burst, resealed. Pus flowed like hot honey, dried up. Scabs fell off, the skin underneath pushing outwards, pink, new, fleshy algae blooming. His mouth gaped wide as he watched his own fingers grow back, toes too. Each digit reformed with excruciating speed, filling his entire being with the kind of pain he thought people could only write about, never experience.

A delicate boot clicked nearby, stopping mere inches from his nose as it sprouted from the melted remains of his face. Unable to help himself, Garrett tried to look at Anna through new eyes, his vision blurred as the white goo of his eyeballs solidified into solid orbs once again, as his corneas regrew, as his pupils contracted as if for the very first time.

And there she stood, emerging from the haze looking like a giant from where he lay on the floor of the bar, that lighter in her hand, another printout in the other.

"No more," he sobbed, a broken man. "No more, I'm sorry. I'm sorry Anna."

"No, you're not," she replied, coldly. She unfolded the image, this one taken in the back of his red pickup truck. She was sweaty, gagged, eyelashes clumped from her mascara running. There were several other people in this photo, none of whom she had consented to. Ropes of white lay across locks of her hair, her clothes.

The lighter clicked.

"Nooooo!" Garrett screamed. His body lifted itself from the floor with the force of the fire reborn.

Anna watched him burn, head cocked lightly to one side.

"Forever, remember?" she said, holding the picture out in front of her. "And the good news is there are plenty more where this came from. You made sure of that, didn't you?"

Garrett, suspended in midair, mid flame, mid pain, mid demise, forever, a picture never fully burned or erased, could not, did not answer.

Anna spoke for him, hair still standing right up on end, as if she were running an electric current through herself, as if lightning ran in her veins. Her eyes were fire-bright, terrifying.

"Aww," she said, as Garrett burned, caught eternally between one life and the next with no escape possible, because, as he'd so eloquently put it, *ain't no wiping that shit away once it's out there*, "honey, I'm sorry. Look what you made me do!"

Garrett's body began to contract, curl into a fetal position, the extreme heat tightening his muscles, making him shrink in on himself. He wondered, distantly, as his flesh bubbled and burned, as his ears melted, as his limbs contorted and his teeth cracked in the heat, how long she could keep this going for.

"As long as I want to," she said, smiling broadly as the third picture curled and vanished into the fire. She patted her pocket happily, and Garrett could see through the flames, before they took his eyes from him once more, softening them like runny eggs, her pocket was fat with folded printouts, stuffed with dozens, if not hundreds of pictures to burn.

Marjorie

By Nathan Buck

Bracelets of colored beads glimmer and catch the sun. Laughter curves around the birch tree where the piñata hangs, and onto the back porch, and all over me. Folding chairs get overturned, and soda is spilled from plastic cups onto the plastic tablecloths. Children's hands rummage through the red cooler and empty it, dropping ice cubes back in before they melt underneath the midsummer sun. Dad runs to the shed to grab more cans, bottles, cartons. The tiki torches keep out most of the mosquitoes; two bite my neck, only five minutes and an inch apart. Four wasps stick their legs into a glob of frosting on the grass. A lost pink barrette ends up in a bed of dandelions. A dress is caught and ripped on a thorn in my mother's garden. Two boys smear dirt on each other's shirts and in each other's hair as they wrestle. Freckles, braces, awkward growth spurts. My sister Ali tears apart wrapping paper and tears open envelopes and casts the remnants onto the lawn like confetti taken for granted.

I'm in charge of passing out slices of chocolate cake with scoops of goopy vanilla ice cream on the side. Ali's decked out in her black-and-white dress just like she promised, looking ready for brand-new wisdoms that arrive with twelve-year-olds and birthday parties, but I can't put my finger on how those revelations work their way under the skin once you blow out your birthday candles. Mom and Dad aim for casual parental control: slacks, short-sleeved button-ups, sandals. They're both tall drinks of water. Runs in the family. I'm wearing shorts, suddenly embarrassed by my pasty legs in front of Ali's friends even though they're all three and four years younger than me.

Time for the piñata. Dad was worried about stripping the bark, so he'd strung the jump rope-turned-noose carefully from the birch's widest branch. No more jumping now. He'd used a knife to cut off the handles, serrated like the tree's legion of triangular leaves. The piñata's about two feet long and a foot wide. I think it's got wings, but those could be arms, even tentacles. And are those feet or fins or talons? Black eyes rest above what I gather is a beak, with a tongue or fang jutting out from the side. Feathers or scales line the papier-mâché body. It's like the piñata's fitted together from a dozen different ideas breach-birthed by a demented toymaker.

Last Wednesday evening, Mom went against type, hurrying off in a tizzy then returning with the piñata laid bare in the trunk of our Subaru. She chose to show me and only me right then. "Got it from the Olde Curiosity Shoppe off the capitol square," she'd said all hushed, as if we were talking ransoms and kidnappings. "Their business card claims, 'Healing the Broken-Hearted & Near-Empty,' so we'll see." I'd never heard of the shop nor the ramifications of its motto. Mom claims it's all right there for the taking.

She said that bells jingled as she walked into the shop, but she didn't note any bells garlanding the ornate, gothic entrance. Wooden shelves lined the walls, where dolls and stuffed animals stared her down with beady marble eyes. None were slumped over, no heads even tilted to the side. On the floor, a train sat silently on its track, this close to getting swallowed by a snowcapped mountain. A bouncing ball rested against a rack filled with vintage picture books.

Dozens of piñatas hung from the ceiling, swaying and bumping into one another: donkeys, unicorns, dragons, peacocks, penguins, dogs, dolphins, fairies, eagles, five-pointed stars, even the earth itself. Ropes were intertwined with ribbons to hold the piñatas three feet from the ceiling, while scattered clusters of loose ribbons dangled free of sold piñatas or new ones not brought out for display yet. The shopkeeper told Mom that he'd used marionette strings until just a couple years back, but patrons kept snagging fingers or even their whole hands in the invisible strings and he'd have to cut them down, restring them later. He told her, "The ropes give strength, but the ribbons breathe life."

Now, Ali's classmates gather round her in a Ring-Around-the-Rosie circle minus holding hands. She tucks her hair behind her ears. I hand the blindfold to my father then step behind Jared Hackle, who's wiping his glasses clean with his T-shirt. Mom sets down a stack of boardgames then joins me stage left of the tree. The air, so still. From this angle, I definitely see the curve of wings. The eyes of the avian-like creature are closed. The talons look ready for perching or carrying away prey to its end. Jared Hackle adjusts his glasses on the rim of his nose.

Dad draws the blindfold across Ali's eyes and ties a knot in back. Stacy Olds and Sharon Ross clap their hands. Dad spins my sister around three times then guides her to a stop. Vertigo slaps her, she loses balance. He steadies her, hands her the cracked and stained baseball bat he's held onto with pride since he was her age.

Mollie Keeper asks, "Should we sing Happy Birthday again?" But Ali's gripping and raising the bat straight out in front of her.

Somebody sneezes. Most everybody blesses them, including me. Ali swings once, misses, twice, misses again. On her third try, the bat whacks the bird. I flinch. Yes, it's for sure a bird. But I don't know what kind yet. It knocks against the underside of the branch, caught in a shadow that dapples it gray. Then back into the sun, into bright white. A muffled rustling inside its stomach. What types of candies are going to spill out? Did the shopkeeper fill it or did Mom? Stacy Olds claps, just once. Mom says, "That's my girl," kind of quiet, and maybe I'm the only one who hears. The wings settle, no more ruffling.

Mollie Keeper's turn. Three misses. Out of luck. Harry McLachlan strikes on his first try. The piñata doesn't crack. The blindfold switches from face to face, knotted, loosened, knotted again. Our backs, chests, and armpits sweat and drip and stain and stick to our shirts. We're cocooned inside this thick Wisconsin humidity.

Sharon Ross admits she can peek out from the bottom. "I'm no cheater," she insists, so Dad readjusts it.

The bird sways, knocks, jangles, won't burst. Someone mentions chocolate. I count the fourteen guests' heads, their forty-two swings.

My turn. The back of the blindfold's scratchy against my eyelids, like sand between your toes. A lash gets wedged in one corner, and I tear up then blink it away as Dad spins me and I go all dizzy. I close my eyes and sparks dance; I strike out.

Mom swings, swings, hits while I stare at her cherry-red fingernails. Whispers congeal—*Why won't the piñata break?*—then Mom knots the blindfold for Dad. He cracks then cracks then cracks the weapon against the bird. Whispers bleed into worry. The wings almost flap, but that must be light and shadows weaving. There aren't even any fractures. Dad mutters, "What the hell?", and Ali bites her lip, ready to start crying, and Dad finally whips off the blindfold and smacks, smacks, smacks. The metal hook twists, ready to snap. Mom wraps her arms around Ali from behind. Everyone else moves in closer then freezes, trapped in still life. The bird settles, still as stone.

Ali's hands are tucked beneath her face as if she's pulling a prayer in close. She's lying on her bed, facing the doorway. Her bedroom door's only halfway open, so I can't see anything to my right past the headboard.

"Go away, Austin," she says, curling her legs up to her chest. One kneecap rests on a purple square of quilt. Ali's wearing cotton pants and a tank top now, all bones and gangly angles. Silver rings circle both of her pinkie toes: stars and crescent moons.

"I'll only stay a second, promise." I flip my palms up, shrug. "I won't mention the piñata disaster."

She raises her head, hair shifting over maroon and golden squares. Grandma Marjorie knitted this patchwork quilt for our mother's twenty-first birthday. "Next year's going to be different. How I feel, I mean. Being a teenager and everything. I just wanted today to go perfect. So I won't ever forget."

"About being a kid?"

She says, "Brains are funny. I don't remember things how they happen. It's like I stamp memories with weird colors."

I step into the room and see her beanbag pushed up under the window, her favorite spot for reading. Deep amber covers the entire sky, dusk untouched on either side by day or night. The birch tree's branches claw upwards. The piñata is far out of view below the windowsill.

"If I'm in a black-and-white mood," Ali continues, "I might see things as totally bright or totally dark, with a line right down the center. Those moods are easiest, when I can divide, pretend life's a math problem. But if I'm in a red mood, angry or embarrassed, then I can look back on something ordinary, even eating breakfast with you and Mom every morning, and it's like my brain's bleeding. Nothing stays in the lines. And I get all sad."

I close the distance and sit on the bed. Ali has laid some of her presents in a straight line against the headboard: a chained dolphin pendant, a hardcover edition of Madeleine L'Engle's *A Wrinkle in Time*, and a CD one of her friends burned for her. The see-through jewel case lets me read the title written in black Sharpie right on the CD itself, *Boys of Summer*.

I've got a secret boyfriend this summer and all year round. Patrick Lillard's a grade ahead of me. We sit at different cafeteria tables when school's in session. He sits with the other jocks and preps while I hunker down with fellow nerds at the opposite end of the spectrum. Patrick rock climbs like a pro, and I can barely toss a stone into a pond and cause any ripple effects whatsoever. He goes to classmates' parties on the weekends while I rent movies with my parents then stay up way too late reading literary classics running the gamut from Ray Bradbury to Shirley Jackson to Daphne du Maurier. Patrick's mom and dad go out on a dinner-and-movie date every Thursday to *keep the romance alive*, so we know he can let me in through the sliding door off the back patio then upstairs to his room those days.

But here's the thing: Patrick doesn't like getting naked in front of me whenever we have sex. So even though I go for broke almost always and strip down to my birthday suit, he keeps his wife-beaters on and pulls his jeans or shorts down only just enough to get the job done. Sometimes he even leaves his socks and shoes on, like he wants to get the hell away from me lickety-split right after we're done cleaning up our mess.

Ali catches me looking at the CD and sits all the way up, curls falling across both cheeks, then pulls a makeup kit out from under the pillow.

"From Delilah Kirkland." She waves the kit so things rattle and clatter inside. "Mom wants me to wait till high school to wear lipstick and eye shadow."

Except for playing dress-up when she was a little girl, the most makeup I've ever seen Ali wear is lip gloss. But in two years she'll have mastered the art. Boys will come calling to impress our parents and tell Ali how pretty she looks. She'll learn to flirt in public and introduce boyfriends to our family.

I shift on the mattress, and Ali's presents shift with me. The dolphin rolls across an edge of envelope and knocks against a corner of the jewel case. I ask, "What color did today end up being?" Part of me's rabbit-holing elsewhere. I can only pick an immovable gray zone to shine a spotlight on whatever's going on between Patrick and me.

Sure, he's ashamed of being into other guys, and we can't hang out when we're around other people. But he always sticks up for me in the hallway if other kids call me *faggot*. He even shoved Tommy Doyle into a locker once and told him if he heard that word again he'd smash Tommy's nose in. Tommy hasn't called me a fag since. Patrick doesn't pick on anyone else either, and he volunteers three times a week in the Special Ed classroom, where he tutors the kids who are slower than the rest of us and need someone to read to them or help them solve their math homework. Some of the Special Ed kids look way different than the rest of us. One boy has a deformed face, and one girl's fingers are webbed together. Patrick told me this other guy—his name is Michael or Mitchell, I can't remember—has something wrong with his throat and needs to be fed through a tube in his stomach by one of the teacher's aides.

Ali answers me. "My birthday started out black and white. But then the piñata didn't break, and it turned burning red. Now, I don't know if I even felt those colors or if afterwards I covered up the hours with them and buried them." She glances out the window then at the makeup kit, probably wondering what colors are inside, how long it will take her to get life just right.

I remember how Uncle Chuck was babysitting me on the day my parents brought little newborn Ali home from the hospital. When they walked through the door, my uncle handed me a pillow with a pattern of stitched roses, and I sat in the living room armchair. Uncle Chuck pressed the pillow into my stomach, and my mom lowered Ali into my lap, keeping her hands on my sister's shoulders, and I stared at Ali's wrinkled prune face. I stroked her tiny hand, let her clamp my pinkie. My feet dangled several inches above the floor, one shoelace undone and touching the carpet.

The piñata stirs even though there's no wind. My socks grow damp from the dew on the grass in our backyard. I swear I can taste Madison's autumn chill waking me up, a prologue to my next season. I clutch the baseball bat. A screech fills the night. The bird spreads its wings, and life moves in its body. The wings start flapping, scraping leaves. But that's got to be just in my head. The jump rope stretches to its limit on the mangled hook. The string of white lights looped around the branches burns out with a mechanical crack.

The first two strikes won't work. I intuit this, but I embrace the fervor of ritual and belief. And I raise the bat, swing, hit the bird—it cries out in pain. It's an owl, fully formed right before getting blown apart. It's made up its mind to answer the call of this species, strata, and slash of history. Hit it again. It screeches louder, and I catch a glimpse of tongue. The owl slams against the trunk, a blur of feathers striking bark. Trails of black blood splash through the air, an artist's paintbrush gone haywire. My palms itch. There's a drip, drip, dripping down past me onto the grass: I pray it's dewdrops losing their grip from tree leaves.

"You're so alive," I gasp. To the owl. To myself.

Steady my hips, narrow my eyes. Swing the bat one final time. Smash the owl in its chest. A ripping of flesh. Next comes release. Hundreds of scraps of paper spill out, pooling together on the ground. A death rattle echoes, spittle and phlegm trapped between lungs and throat, systems failing.

When I bend down to get a closer look, clear moonlight reveals clean edges. I sort through every piece of paper. They're grocery store receipts. White or yellowed, typed or handwritten, folded or crumpled or pressed flat, they span eras and technologies from the last century. They all hail from Minnesota, where Mom grew up, and they're all signed *Marjorie*. No last name, as if she's the one and only. And to me, she is. My grandmother's signature is deliberate. The letters of her name bear clean edges too, no smears or swirls crossing the line.

Who did this and why? How'd they get ahold of all of these? I can't shake the feeling the receipts weren't "gotten" at all. They manifested right here, caged or sheltered inside the belly of the bird. *Healing the Broken-Hearted & Near-Empty*. My mother invited these intentions.

We'd visited Grandma Marjorie in Duluth seven or eight times a year. Grandpa Rob died of lung cancer when Mom was pregnant with me, and my grandmother loved our company. Ali and I always complained on the car ride going both ways. After we arrived, I'd resist the urge to pluck off the white and gray and brown feathers from the fourteen taxidermied owls mounted on the walls, beckoning from the living room and hallways and up the stairs. I wanted to cut holes into their chests and bellies to witness what was kept sacred inside.

When I was six years old, just a few months shy of Grandma Marjorie dying in her sleep, I found myself standing at the only owl in her living room, the Snowy one. It was perched on this gnarled piece of wood hooked onto the wall, and I stroked its closed beak, wondering if it still had its tongue or if owls even had tongues in the first place. Unannounced, Grandma Marjorie showed up behind me—I caught that overkill whiff of her hairspray—and she whispered, "You wouldn't think there's a plastic frame under there." She took over, stroking the owl's left wing and back, then added, "The taxidermist only uses part of the skeleton, you know. Just enough to give the skin its proper shape. It's not like the old days, when they stuffed things with straw." I should've asked her questions about her olden days, but I looked away from the owl instead, disappointed it didn't have any real body parts left inside, and I focused on the dark stains on the wall.

In the years since Mom and Dad sold my grandparents' house, I've wondered if those stains came from Grandpa Rob's smoking and if my grandmother left them as a remnant of his love, even if it meant remembering what killed him.

Right now, the owl stops swaying, so I reach up and yank on the papery flesh. The hook snaps and the owl falls, landing several feet away from me. The curl of jump rope—tangled between its talons—reaches toward its neck. The black eyes remain open, glassy and slick yet impenetrable like twin crystal balls.

My childhood owls had always stared unblinking, their eyelids glued open for eternity. What died didn't stay dead. Never does. A couple years ago, I'd gone down to our basement and peeked through the storage boxes marked *GM* for Grandma Marjorie but only found Hummels, antique jewelry, porcelain china, and the silk scarves my grandmother collected but never wore. Everything was packed tightly within folds of newspaper, gauze, and bubble wrap. Are the owls down there in other boxes I haven't discovered yet? Did Mom sell them at a garage sale or to an antique dealer after Grandma Marjorie crossed the veil?

Whenever I think about the owls, I remember how Grandma Marjorie baked German pancakes and wore an apron with that pretty flower pattern while candles burned in the kitchen alcove. She'd talk to Ali and me about kindness versus cleverness, politeness versus power, and when to wield which. I remember the wrinkly, soft skin of her hands that reminded me of well-loved bookmarks, and a black-and-white picture of Mom as a teenager hanging over her double bed, and her crackly laugh that Mom always joked sounded like milk being poured over Rice Krispies.

I sense the shadow behind me. My mother rests a hand on my shoulder. "What are you doing out here, Austin?"

"I wanted to break it open." I point to the Snowy Owl. "It couldn't wait till morning."

She tilts her head, moving slowly toward the fallen creature without examining the receipts or looking around for scattered candy. Then she scoops up the owl, untangles the jump rope, drops it, and shivers as if she'd been holding intestines spilled out of a wound in its gut.

"Your father's program won't last forever," she says. "We'd better hurry."

She leads me behind the birch tree, further back, no, further, past the mound of dog's mercury. I used to believe it was a faeries' den, an altar where miniature beings practiced magic. But then Mom informed me the plants were poisonous and would've killed any other living thing who worshipped there.

We kneel side by side, hidden from our neighbors by a lone elm towering on their side of the picket fence. Mom sets the owl out of sight then points down, identifying an invisible marker. We rip the grass with our hands, clawing out chunks of soil. The dirt feels warm and cold at the same time somehow. My heart slows enough to hear crickets chirping and cicadas buzzing for the first time tonight. Where are the lightning bugs? I haven't laid eyes on even one single neon blink. Clearly, they're wise enough to not illuminate anything more than I need shown here. My fingers brush against earthworms, my nails click against stones.

After a few minutes, we uncover the lid of a wooden crate with slats too close together for me to see inside. Mom frees the crate and brushes its sides, dirt crumbling away. Then she rips off the lid. The crate's empty inside.

She looks at me for the longest time then says, "I miss my parents. I haven't been to visit them in years. I'm sure all the flowers wilted and blew away a long time ago. And the grass probably grew in weird patches around the Virgin Mary that's next to her tombstone. Have you ever noticed that? How the grass right over graves looks splotchier than the rest of cemetery lawns? You know I'm not religious, but your grandmother was, and I wanted to honor her. Your Grandpa Rob always did the same. He went to church, took communion, the whole bit, even though his side of the family's just two-timer Catholics, his words. The Christmas and Easter kind, with a wedding or funeral thrown in now and then for good measure."

I wish I had even one Grandpa Rob memory, but all I get are old photo albums. He's this tall man in sepia who wore tweed coats, slicked his hair back, and sometimes wore glasses. He's this boy with a gap in his teeth standing near a fence and cornfield. He's two-dimensional fiction. Weird to think of him dying the same month I was conceived, like we met somewhere coming and going in some form we won't quite recall until we're at that crossroads again.

Mom continues, "Whenever I left to visit them, you cupped your hands around your eyes when I kissed you and Ali and your dad goodbye at the door. Do you even remember that? It's like you were clicking a View-Master, moving the disk from slide to slide, deciding how to capture me until I got back. I tapped into a frequency of peace kneeling there in La Dame Cemetery. Like I wasn't alone. I wouldn't call it God, but if I didn't know better, I'd say it was a song only I could hear, a circuit of verses opening and closing, again and again. Lyrics about my parents and what it felt like to literally look up to them, when I stood as tall as their hips and they both seemed as infinite as the sky, plucking their backlogged dreams from the clouds to leave to me."

I wonder if there's a third empty plot, reserved long ago, just in case Mom changes her mind about religion. She's an only child and self-proclaimed atheist who wants to be cremated, her ashes taken across town and cast into the lakes past where our feet could touch.

She moves toward tonight's ending and says, "Growing up, the three of us attended mass every Sunday, rain or shine, sick or pretending to be. And every week after church, my father lit a cigar and walked the mile home. My mother hustled me into our Buick Skylark and forced me to go grocery shopping. We'd meticulously, even religiously, travel every single aisle in the mart like clockwork. Then we'd go home and spend the afternoon preparing a magnificent supper. My parents took turns picking out records from classical to doo-wop for us to listen to after we said grace. I should've asked her how to be in this world and to write it all down, but instead I moved to Minneapolis for college and when I came home for the holidays that first winter break and went to church but wouldn't take communion, well, she didn't ask me any questions either. Not then and not after I dropped out and moved back to Duluth and stopped going to mass altogether."

She looks to my far side. "Now hand me that owl."

I obey. My fingers sink into the thick, downy feathers. Avoiding its glorious stare—the transfiguration complete—Mom places the Snowy Owl in the crate. I retrieve the pile of receipts then go back to make sure I don't miss any strays. We cloak God's creature with every scrap taken from my mother and now gifted back, a paper trail of grace and faith. She seals the crate and lowers it back into the ground. Then we pile on heaps of dirt, making sure to spread it flat. Mom takes my hand, little clods of dirt getting pressed between our palms. Part of me wants to trick myself into believing I know better, but the truth wins out. Grandma Marjorie is still around; she's singing to us now. After a couple minutes I sit upright, realizing I'd leaned down and rested my head on my mom's shoulder. Her bones have left a mark on my cheek. The impression slowly fades.

I Look In People's Windows

By Todd Keisling

"Good evening, lonely travelers. It's your old pal Gus here, talkin' to y'all on this fine October evening from the comfort of my studio. I've got my coffee and a cigarette, the candles are burning, and if I squint the right way, the Lexington skyline looks just like a sea of stars. From now until the break of dawn, it's just us and the strange stories the Southland allows us to tell. And believe me, listeners, I have a doozy for you tonight..."

—Gus Guthrie, *Midnight in the Southland* radio broadcast, October 8th, 1999

Our memories are so strange, aren't they? They're these little windows we keep in our minds, framing moments we've chosen to keep locked away and brimming with all manner of mysteries we couldn't see at the time. Sometimes, we close their curtains; sometimes, we find them again, and gaze through them on a whim. I'm talking about the way a sound, a scent, or a turn of phrase can unlock something in our heads, pulling back the curtain on some dusty window you didn't even know was there. But what happens when you aren't prepared for the multitudes a memory might contain? What happens when you've locked it away and closed the curtain for good reason?

Well, a racist curmudgeon once wrote, "Unhappy is he to whom the memories of childhood bring only fear and sadness." He isn't wrong, listeners. I can't speak for everyone out there in the Southland tonight, but I'd hazard a guess that many of you lonely travelers can relate. I certainly can. I locked those unhappy memories away so long ago that I'd forgotten they were even there.

Hell, listen to me. You're all probably thinking, "What's got Gus so maudlin tonight?" It's the date, friends. The date, and something I saw that's got me shook.

Folks here in Lexington probably heard about the arrest that occurred on the other side of Woodhill last night. A homeless man was arrested for allegedly trespassing on private property. Happens all the time, right? Here's where it gets a little strange. The man—who has yet to be identified—was described as having "sallow, sagging skin and empty, hollow eyes." Their words, folks. But what's more intriguing is this detail: He wore tattered denim overalls covered in coal dust and a cap that read "Paxton Mining Co."

Now, I'm not sure what's stranger: that he wore a hat for a mining operation that's been out of business for almost seventy years, or that he had a bouquet of wildflowers in his hand. No ID. No fingerprints on record. This man wandered out of the night, right out of time, and into someone's backyard where he stood peering through their living room window. One other detail I forgot to mention: he was crying tears of black. Soot, probably, from whatever coal vein he climbed out of, but I'm not so sure. It's one more mystery for the archives, I s'pose. That's how things go here in the Southland, don't they?

Anyway, I told y'all that story so I could tell you this one. See, the name Paxton rang a bell for me, and reminded me of some trouble I got up to when I was young, something I've not thought about in decades. I guess there're some memories we don't necessarily want to bury. They just slip from our consciousness and fall into the ruts of time—until we trip over something sticking out of the mud, something we didn't see because we were too focused on what's ahead.

For me, it was yesterday's date: October 8th, 1999. It was the branded cap for Paxton, and the black tears.

Unhappy is he, indeed. Let's be honest with ourselves, listeners. What's a Southland story without a little sorrow?

There was plenty of it around these parts back in '58, with an ill feeling in the air like something was looming on the horizon none of us could see. The coal industry was dryin' up. Tobacco was on the decline. People were pullin' up stakes to go find work in the cities, and poverty was the rule, not the exception.

My family wasn't safe from the economic hardship. We lived on Mama's family farm with my Papaw Earl, a stalwart fellow who helped raise me when my folks were at each other's throats, which I recall was often. Daddy was a drinker, had been for as long as I can remember, and he hated farming. He never told me so, not directly, but he didn't have to. Some men have soil in their hearts and green on their thumbs, but not my daddy. He couldn't even grow the corn used in the mash he drank every night.

I was eighteen that year, should've been off to college but there was no money to go around, so I spent my days working on the farm with Daddy and Papaw. Honest work, but I think I took after my daddy when it came to farming. One of the few things we had in common, I suppose. Then again, we did have a shared love of hunting. That's how we came to be in Harlan on the 8th of October 1958: buck season.

The "Guthrie Family Cabin," as Daddy called it, sat at the foot of Black Mountain and was more like a two-man shed. Just enough room to bed down and store your equipment. Daddy and my uncle Collin had used it since they were little kids, one of the only things their father had left them. Collin died in Korea in '52, and their annual hunting trips died with him.

Color me surprised when he asked if I wanted to go hunting with him that season. I'd been itching to leave the farm for a while, not that I'd ever tell Papaw that, and I jumped at the chance. Looking back, I think Daddy knew he was driving Mama crazy and just wanted to give her a break from his troubles.

The whole drive, he talked about the ten-point buck he was gonna bring home, and how it would feed us for the winter. He was in good spirits, a rarity in those days, and I couldn't help but smile at his happiness. It's how I prefer to think of him now. Wide-eyed with his hands on the wheel, wearing a cocky Guthrie grin framed with a grizzled beard, exuding pure joy...

It was thirty-one years ago, and my hands still shake when I think about it. If I seem emotional, or like I'm beatin' around the bush, it's because I closed the curtain on this memory for a reason.

We arrived in Harlan early that morning, fueled up at the diner in town, and parked at the trailhead. Daddy turned to me and said, "Before we set off, son, I need to tell ya something. You might've been too young to remember the last time we came here, but you're a man now, so you need to be aware of the trail fork."

I asked him what he meant.

"They call this the Paxton trail on account of the old company town along the Cumberland River. It's a ghost town and no one lives there, which means we ain't got no business *going* there. Understand?"

"Sure, Daddy."

I didn't, though, and I think Daddy sensed it because he grabbed my wrist and gave me one of those icy Buford Guthrie stares like I'd crossed him. "I'm serious, son. There's a fork in the trail a few miles up the mountain. We go right, never left. Whole place is probably overgrown by now and it might be hard to tell what's what." He studied me for a moment, and then he said, "Just follow me. And if you hear music, no ya didn't."

The subtle tremor, the intensity in his voice rattled me, made my heart skip a beat. I looked ahead at the Paxton Trail, which was more like a mountain access road, dusty gravel choked with weeds and kudzu. Remains of a bygone era when companies built whole towns to house their workers. Company towns, they called 'em, with their own currency known as "scrip," which was just another way of enslaving the poor to work for the rich. There were a few such companies before the Harlan coal wars in the 30s, and in its day, Paxton was the largest.

Sat on the shores of the Cumberland River some fifteen miles east of Harlan. The Paxton brothers set up shop in the late 1800s to tap a coal vein that many surveyors said wasn't there. The brothers proved them all wrong, though, and at the height of production, Paxton Mining Co. employed and housed over twelve thousand workers.

There's speculation over how the brothers found the vein, especially considering surveyors disagreed with their assessment. What few news articles I could dig up in the station archives reference a "trade secret" both Arlo and James Paxton coyly mentioned to the press, but the truth behind said "secret" was never divulged. Anyone who knew that truth is long gone now, likely buried at the bottom of the mine. It collapsed in 1928, and again in 1929 with the stock market. The Paxton Family's wealth seemingly vanished overnight, and the fiefdom they'd built for themselves in Harlan County quickly crumbled. No one really knows what happened to Arlo and James after that. Historians believe they retired from the industry and set off for parts unknown.

I wouldn't be telling y'all this if it had no bearing, and I share this brief history of Paxton to set the stage for what came next on our journey to the family cabin.

We reached the fork in a couple of hours. Daddy paused long enough to kick a strand of kudzu from a fallen sign. "This way to Paxton," the sign read in chipped lettering. He stared on down the gravel road for a moment, his head tilted to the side, listening. I didn't hear anything but the sounds of the forest and the nearby Cumberland River, but something had caught his ear, and I stood there in silence watching him. He shook his head, mouthed something I couldn't make out, and turned back to me.

"Let's go," he said. I wanted to ask him about his warning, why there might be music coming from the place if it was a ghost town, but then he was on his way, taking a right from the fork. I never asked him about it. Wish I had, though. Never got the chance again.

Daddy pointed out some deer droppings along the way, certain that we'd have a bountiful hunt in the coming days, but there was a slight hitch in his voice. Something had spooked him back at the fork and he was trying to hide it. His hands shook whenever he took out his hip flask, and I caught him looking over his shoulder more than once.

There *was* something in the air, though. I couldn't put my finger on it then, and I'm not sure I can now. Everything was still, like the whole mountainside was either dead or simply afraid to move. That time of year, we should've heard the scuttling of squirrels in the fallen leaves and quarreling of birds in the trees, but there was only the breeze and its cold bite. I've replayed this in my head over the years, questioning my memories of the feeling, if maybe it wasn't tension or unease but Daddy's alcoholism getting the better of him. No matter how I shake it, the fact remains: Daddy was scared even if he'd never admit it, and his fear fueled my own.

And no wonder, really. The Guthrie Cabin sat in Black Mountain's shadow, half-buried in foliage, its roof carpeted with moss. It was only an hour's hike from the fork, the trail snaking the mountain rim, and we felt the cool October chill with every step. The structure was more rundown than I remembered, its timbers rotten, the one tiny window fractured. I remember thinking it looked how I always imagined the witch's hut from Grimms' *Hansel and Gretel*.

Daddy didn't say much after we arrived. We unpacked our things, set up camp, and made a fire to cook our dinner. He spent most of the evening sitting outside, watching the sun slowly crawl to the west. After dark, I joined him by the fire, stretched out, and gazed up at the stars.

When you're in the dark like that, your mind wanders into strange places, crossing into territories you never thought you'd venture. The sky wasn't like it is now, littered with satellites. That night in the wilderness

I saw the cosmos unfiltered, a whole belt of stars and planets swirling across the infinite, and I pondered how infinitely small we are in the scheme of everything. We're just observers, I realized, looking up and looking in, maybe looking in places we aren't meant to see. We never think about what might be looking back at us from the other side—even from a window of memory.

I must've drifted off to sleep, because when I opened my eyes, the flames were low and Daddy was gone. I lay there for a time, recollecting where I was and why I was outside, when a jarring strum of guitar strings slipped loose from the forest. I sat up with a jolt and held my breath, praying I was dreaming, because what I'd heard, listeners, was something like music. Old time music, the kind you might hear warbling from a warped record. Scratched and fuzzy with static from a worn needle. "Shady Grove," by the sound, but the singer's voice was distorted at half-speed and transformed the folk song into a dirge of sorrow.

Shaaaaady grooooove, myyyy littleeee looooove...

Daddy's admonition should have prepared me for it, but I'll tell you, listeners, those dissonant notes echoing in the air gave me the willies in the worst way. I'd grown up hearing all sorts of stories about the region, the haints that haunted the Appalachian foothills, the peculiar families deep in the hollers who didn't take kindly to outsiders. Old folk tales, you know? I'd never heard anything about Paxton until that morning. It was just another town to me, one Daddy didn't want me visiting. And because this is me, listeners, y'all know I'm the curious type. One of the reasons Daddy and I never got along, to be honest. I was always sticking my nose where it didn't belong.

I checked the cabin. Daddy wasn't there, and neither was his hunting rifle. I took my own rifle and flashlight, whispered a prayer, and headed back down the trail. I'd walked for ten minutes without any sign of my father, and against my better judgment, I called out to him in the dark.

Nothing. The forest was silent but for the haunting song crawling through the air.

I'mm bouuuund toooo goooo awaaaayyy...

"Daddy?" I called again, and the song kept droning on in reply. *He's probably drunk*, I told myself. Maybe the old fool wandered off into the dark, slipped and fell into a pile of leaves. Maybe he was sleeping off the booze and none the wiser to the ghostly melody.

But I knew better. He'd been strange ever since we crossed the fork earlier that day. The whole drive to Harlan, he could barely contain his excitement for the hunt. Once we got to the fork, he'd clammed up. Kept looking over his shoulder, tilting his head like he could hear something I couldn't.

And there I was, wandering through the forest in pitch darkness without his guidance. A lonely traveler shining a light into the unknown. I thought I knew darkness back on the farm, but the wilderness humbled me that night. The sky was overcast and stingy with moonlight. If not for my flashlight, I couldn't see my hand in front of my face. Didn't let it stop me from going on. All I could think about was Mama and how she'd tan my hide for losing Daddy in the woods. It never occurred to me what she might think if I got lost, too.

The record scratched, cutting the song mid-lyric, and silence settled into the darkness, into my bones. A moment later, I heard the subtle pops of static as the needle hit the groove of a new record, but no music followed. No sound at all, listeners. The record was blank, or seemed to be. These days I'm not so sure.

My journey brought me back to the fork, and from there I glimpsed strange lights down the gravel path toward Paxton. Pale blue flashes like heat lightning, but the chill down my back betrayed my eyes. Early October in those days had a bite in the air. Whatever flashed in the Paxton wasn't of nature.

Had Daddy ignored his own advice and gone into the town? Had someone taken him? Or was I the fool, wandering alone into the dark wilderness while my father slept off a drunken stupor? There's not a day goes by that I don't wonder about the circumstances and what transpired in the short time I slept, but I knew the moment I saw those lights I'd find him there.

Ghostly static sizzled through the woods as I approached. I wasn't stealthy, had no intention of trying to hide my advance, and expected to encounter someone who'd tell me to leave. I'd brought my own rifle just in case of such a standoff, but to my surprise, there was no guard, and I received no warning. My entrance to Paxton was unceremonious, as empty as the spaces in the dark, and I was greeted by hissing static from speakers affixed to electrical poles. Energy arced across bare wires, surging in erratic patterns and lighting up the night. Pale blue flashes cast leaning, rotten houses in silhouette.

Some of the homes still retained their windows, and in the light's erratic flashing, I glimpsed gaunt figures looking back from beyond the glass. Sagging faces and dead, dead eyes. Dark tears trickled down their soot-coated cheeks. I drew close to one window and peered inside. They were miners, or had been once upon a time, still wearing their dusty overalls and carbide helmets.

Immovable statues, each staring into empty space, until one of them met my gaze. A vast, empty sorrow communicated across the distance between us and filled my heart with such a loneliness that I struggle now to explain it. How long had these men been separated from their loved ones? And what unholy bond had held them here for all these years?

For that moment the forest fell still, the seething static muted, and the world of the derelict cabin slowly crawled into focus. Had all these men been here before I looked inside? I imagined them packed into these derelict homes, waiting for someone to come along and peek inside, someone to *see* them. Waiting for *me*.

The moment passed with an exhale, my breath fogging up the dingy window. I stepped away, stunned into silence as movement stirred within. One by one, they exited their shacks and formed a single-file line that wound its way deeper into town.

One by one, they shuffled down the gravel path in lockstep like an army on the march.

Voices hummed from somewhere in town. Something like chanting, but I couldn't make out the words. I joined the procession as the last man in line, not so much out of curiosity but as though I was compelled to do so. I can't really explain it, listeners. It's like the closer I drew to Paxton, the more that blank record began to speak to me, even if I couldn't hear a single word it said.

I followed the miners into town square, and here's where reality's fabric began to loosen for me. I've spoken of this before about the Southland, often from personal experience in my travels since that day, of places where the stitches have come loose. Secret towns, secret highways, filled with secret people and their secret smiles. Places that feel less real and more like a dream.

Paxton was one of them, listeners. But if it was a dream, it was the worst sort. My mind screamed for me to stop, to turn tail and run back to the cabin, to forget Daddy and save myself from the dread suffocating me in that cool October night. Yet I kept walking, clutching my flashlight like a holy relic, praying to the old gods to deliver me from this shifting phantasmagoria.

The gods weren't watching, but *they* were.

Two men in overcoats and bowler hats stood at the end of the road, framed by the archway of a crumbling façade that might have once been a town hall. Before them, a stone pedestal, and upon it sat a small figurine surrounded in a blue glow. The procession of miners split off into two groups, each one lining the square, leaving me standing alone in the center of the street.

I wasn't the only one, though. Knelt before the pedestal was another man, slumped to one side, a rifle slung over his shoulder. Whatever spell had come over me eased up, freeing me to race ahead to my father's side. None of the Paxton men made to stop me.

"Gus," Daddy hissed. "What the hell're you doin' here? Didn't I tell you ..."

"We gotta get out of here, Daddy. This place ain't right—"

One of the hatted men stepped forward. "He is ours."

"Contract," said the other, spoken with a dour southern lilt. "In trade."

"Gus, you tell your mama I love her. Tell 'er I said to move on."

I clutched Daddy's jacket, tried my best to pull him to his feet, but he wouldn't budge. He looked me square in the eye, and the fear I saw staring back turned my guts to lead. *Daddy*, I thought, *what did you do?*

"Just go 'fore they change their minds. Go on 'n git, boy. Mind your daddy." He climbed to his knees and reached for the pedestal, the glowing figure on display. A nasty-looking humanoid figure with hands pressed to its ears, entwined in something like roots, or maybe they were snakes. I didn't get a better look—my eyes were glassy with tears, and I'd already turned to run.

I got as far as the entrance before a final flash of light split the sky. An instant later, the world fell silent. No static, no music, and no chanting. I was alone, and I think if I'd gone back, I would've found the town empty of souls. I stumbled back through the forest, up the mountain trail to the Guthrie cabin, where I collapsed in a heap of tears and terror.

The next morning, I packed up our things, and made my way back into Harlan. Called Mama first, then walked down to the police station to report what had happened. Lot of good it did—the chief smiled grimly and said people go missing around there all the time. He didn't even offer to organize a search, like it was just another day in Harlan, and Daddy's disappearance was as normal as birds in the sky.

I never went back to the mountain cabin. Never went back to Paxton, either, though I admit I got the itch a few times over the years. I've been to all sorts of haunted hollers and ghost towns since that night, but not Paxton. Daddy's warning didn't take at first, but now it's my gospel.

And over the years, I came to forget about that night on Black Mountain. I left the farm, got into radio, and made a life of my own for thirty-one years. Until last night, listeners.

See, that house on the other side of Woodhill was my own. It was my window that Paxton miner was staring through. When I turned on the porch light, when I saw the tear-streaked face of my father looking back at me, the curtains to that horrible memory came fluttering open. His face was coated in soot like he'd been deep in the earth every day for the last three decades.

My neighbor's the one who called the cops. Apparently Daddy had been wandering through several yards before he found me. I don't know how he came to be there, though. He'd died in my heart all those years ago when he'd made a pact with the Paxton men, and the sorrow had always lingered.

I've thought about it all day, about the hatted men and the missing Paxton brothers, about the strange carving to which Daddy had made his pledge. I wonder ... why now? What happened that might've loosed him from their reins?

It's another mystery of the Southland, listeners, one that I'm too afraid to ponder.

But enough of that. I think I've gabbed long enough. Let's go to the phones. Next caller, you're on the air. What brings you out tonight, lonely traveler?

No Body, No Crime

By L.C. Marino

The boat rocks rhythmically beneath us, beneath the star-riddled sky, beneath the swaying pendulum of radiant bone. That brilliant, engorged moon holds my gaze, fills my mind with blissful static. Mother Moon soothes my heart and tempers my blossoming desire to kill.

My prey quivers and squirms under me, his sweat-slicked flesh sliding in my grip. I'm not concerned; he can't escape. He's wrapped in nylon paracord from his neck to his plump, piggy ankles.

"Plump little *castrated* piggy," I say, then snort. I am hilarious when I want to be. I mean, it's true, I did castrate him. I tossed his genitals into the ocean the moment we lost sight of the Long Island shore, his hemorrhaged eyes wide with disbelief as I dropped his stringy testicles into the sea. He couldn't object or fight. I am *fully* in control here. The drugs are working wonderfully.

I could exercise mercy, pierce his trembling body with my last hypodermic needle and administer a final dose of paralytic, but I'd rather wait until he regains some strength. I'll allow a modicum of hope before I pry it from his spirit by depressing the needle's plunger.

My god, this kill is going to be incredible.

I show my face to the moon, to Mother's gift—her radiant love, her protective light guiding me to violence like a lighthouse beam slicing through the dark night to facilitate safe voyage. She whispers their names in my mind as I obsess in her light.

Trina Jenkins.

Jasmine Thomas.

Rhonda Simms.

Lavinia Rodriguez.

Tanisha Don...

She continues, each name coming to me in rhythm with the ocean's swells. Twenty-two daughters of the moon. He took them from us and now I'm charged with setting things right.

"You'll never hurt another daughter. You belong to us now." My dreamy words blend in my mouth, creamy and rich like a caramel promise.

"*Huuuuuu*," he drones, unable to speak but desperate for a voice. I twitch the knife embedded in his gut, sending him into a pitchy whine. Good. That must hurt like hell.

I lean over his face and pin his eyes to the back of his skull with mine before leaning into the blade, a lever to manipulate him, to move him to compliance. He hyperventilates, spittle bubbling on his lips. "You like that, you piece of shit? Is this the same knife you used to carve Trina into ribbons before you dumped her on the dunes? We didn't get a funeral for almost a year after she went missing thanks to you. Her poor mother. This one's for her."

I pull the knife from his gut and drive it into his substantial inner thigh. Bone arrests the blade's momentum just before the hilt reaches his skin. No worries, a little maneuvering will fix that.

His legs kick like a dreaming puppy, his feet twitching on loose ankles just enough to let me know he's suffering but unable to retaliate or defend himself. I've kept him paralyzed for damn near twelve hours. While it's much safer this way, I prefer a more physical, interactive kill. I've never used this much paralytic but Ronald "The Dunes Killer" Jenkins is no ordinary victim. I need him completely disarmed, unable to match or exceed my dominance. He's a large human. A sloppy mass of fifty-year-old muscle and visceral fat. I'm no small fry, but he's gotta have damn near eighty pounds on me. It took every ounce of my strength to wrap him in all this cord, but we got it done, me and Mother Moon.

He's groaning again, traces of a scream buried deep in his incapable body trying its best to grow up and relieve his agony. I hold his frantic gaze.

"I've been hunting you for ten years and you never saw me coming. All this time you assumed you were the only hunter in your orbit. Outside of law enforcement, of course. But we both know they can't get around their own corruption to solve your cases. They're as mired in our world as we are."

I release the knife and swing my legs over his bound form, planting my hands beside his exposed head. His bruises are in bloom, the swelling distorting his normally ugly face into a fairy tale mask. Now fully atop him, I obscure Mother Moon's light, casting new shadows on his mottled terrain.

"I'm just one of them. One of the girls you've been methodically picking off. No one cares about prostitutes, right? Well, *they* care about me and now you do too. I'm the huntress. I'm the Widowmaker Killer."

His eyes stop jittering and swell with realization under their bruised lids. He's fully aware of me, of our overlapping crimes. I'm his equal—a serial killer terrorizing the city's sprawling extremities, littering adjacent killing grounds with my dead.

"That's right. I've been killing vile little boys like you for years. What made you think you were safe? You got too confident, is that it? Ain't no way a little brown girl from Queens could get the upper hand on you, right?"

He scans the space around my face, desperate to deny me this moment of gratification. I won't allow it. I reach between my legs and grip the knife handle.

"Keep your eyes on me or I'm taking my little friend here on another adventure. There's so much left to explore." *Explore.* I *want* to draw the blade. I want the adventure. I crave more carnage.

Mother Moon whispers. *The sea grows impatient, child. Don't keep her waiting. Finish your work. Gain your freedom.*

Waves lap at the hull, gentle but persistent. A breeze licks my exposed skin. Mother is right.

I'm almost free.

I lift my face to his again. His chest swells and drops with each breath. *I'll* end those soon. My privilege is undeniable.

"I'm sorry, Mother. Thank you for this gift."

I close my eyes and press my face into his tacky, blood-streaked cheek and inhale. Something he can't do thanks to the tight wrapping. I smell his fear, its coppery particles penetrating my nostrils, throat, and lungs like a noxious gas. My muscles quake with primal energy. He'll never be in my position again, atop his prey, possessing a life, authorizing death. I consume this privilege in totality.

"A cop gave me your name, you know. I know that cop better than his wife does. They were so close to taking you down. I couldn't let that happen. I couldn't let you get away without real justice."

I press my lips to his open ear, flooding his mind with my words, my breath, my verdict.

"Killers like us crave legacy. I'm rewriting yours tonight. I left a package behind with evidence to connect you to *my* crimes. That's right. You're taking the credit for *my* violence. All those men you killed. What a shame. Who knew you liked guys, too? I wonder what Denise and your sons will think when the press release hits the airwaves. They'll talk about how you tortured those men. Bound and paralyzed them before having your way with them. How you burned them alive and littered the dunes with their ashes. You were really talented. And all the killing ends with your disappearance. Isn't that a coincidence?"

I pull the hypodermic needle from the bag lying beside him like a sleeping cat. He wriggles in protest, knowing what's about to happen. I remove the cap and press the needle into the meat of his neck protruding above the cordage. Then, I weave a loose line of cord around his neck. The line trails to the spool laying on deck beside us. I grab it firmly with my left hand.

"Thanks for taking the fall, asshole." I roll off him, wedge my feet in his side, and shove him into the ocean.

He disappears over the boat's side, plunging into a liquid collision with imminent death. I scramble to the side to watch him drown. I find him just as I'd hoped: partially submerged, his panicked eyes two fully aware shimmering globes inches beneath the surface. He cannot fight. He cannot swim. I lean over the side, my grip tight on the boat rail, my face hovering just above the gentle sea, inches above his desperate gaze.

"Hear those women screaming through me, you rapist, murderous fuck! Know me! *I AM YOUR KILLER!*"

I spin toward the moon, a giddy cackle bubbling in my throat. I drop the cord tethering him to the surface and grab the cool flukes of the spare anchor resting beside me. I hoist it above my head, imagining how sweet it would sound breaching his skull. But there's no appetite for mercy tonight. I wouldn't dream of putting him out of his misery so easily. Instead, I throw the anchor into the darkness just beyond his floating face.

The chain skips and chatters across the metal rail as the anchor blasts through the moon's reflection on the sea. In seconds that chain will chase the anchor into the deep, pulling him with it.

His bloodshot, panicked eyes beg for the mercy he never extended before he's dragged from the surface, into liquid death. He'll spend eternity on the sea floor, suspended by chain, ribbons of flesh and salt-logged bones swaying in the shifting currents.

I laugh so hard I nearly vomit as I collapse onto the pilot's chair, joyous tears cutting rivulets in the salt coating my tacky cheeks. This last kill is orgasmic, pure, unbridled elation. My final act. My denouement.

I repeat our girls' names to Mother Moon one last time before I clutch in the engine and never speak their names again.

Better Than Revenge

By T.W. Piperbrook

Fuck a dish served cold. I want my revenge so hot it sizzles.

I want you to feel the pain that roils in my gut. I want you to burn with the self-loathing that keeps me up night after night, scrutinizing every scar, every blemish, yanking the bra strap that cuts into my shoulder and wishing it would cut me in half. I tug my pale blonde ponytail, wishing the eye-watering sting would strip away my agony. I'd rather die than drag myself through the rest of this wretched life, but I can't leave the world knowing that you two are happy.

And so I think, I observe, and I plan.

I obsess over what makes me unlovable.

My wipers struggle against the downpour, distorting my view as I spy on you through the windshield. Two bodies pressed tightly together under an umbrella, walking the city block. Playfully bumping shoulders. Laughing. Oblivious to the others running frantic circles around you, drenched, rushing for cover. But you? You're always prepared, Rena.

Did you envision this on that first night, when I invited you to the Olympia Diner with Lincoln and me? I should've noticed how his gaze lingered on you, or how tightly you hugged him goodbye. I should've seen that seductive sparkle in your eyes, the one you turn on with the flip of a switch; the one that's charmed so many others. I should've known it then.

You split my soul in half, Rena. You robbed me of every last drop of joy.

You turn a corner and lean close, kissing him. The sight of your locked lips makes me physically ill. He was mine, Rena. *You knew that.*

I should chop off your hands, peel the skin from your flesh and smash your face to a pulp, so you look as ugly as I feel. Carve those sparkling eyes out with a grapefruit spoon and feed them to your fucking goldfish.

I could have stopped this before it started, but I didn't. I trusted you. And now I'm alone.

And you're with him.

Kissing in the rain.

I let my foot off the brake and adjust the two fentanyl patches on my wrists, rolling behind you up the road, wallowing in torment, my vision blurred by rain—or is it tears? I've shed enough to drown this whole dirty city. But no one cares. Not my few pathetic friends, not my mom and dad. Not the server at the coffee shop where Lincoln and I shared our first peppermint mocha, our lips touching the same lid before we even dared hold hands. I still go there, picturing us sitting at the window. Mourning the ghosts of what should have been. Not a single person asks about the pile of damp napkins next to my uneaten Danish or the red rings beneath my eyes.

I'm as invisible now as I was then. My love story with Lincoln was meant for rocking chairs on a rickety porch, a nightly retelling to our grandchildren. Your tale is riddled with lurid lies and betrayal. Were you there the night he told me it was over? Lying next to him, writing the script, whispering the words in his ear that shattered my heart? I should've driven there that night and shoved a stake through yours.

One day—one day *soon*—you'll understand how it feels.

A row of parked cars chokes my view. I take a turn, nearly clipping a sideview mirror as I round the corner, and there you are, taunting me with every carefree step, window-shopping for things you'll never buy, because you've already got it all. Long, silky black hair. Angelic blue eyes. Glowing skin.

Some people are born with everything.

Others are born to take everything away.

I glance at my rearview, and a miserably plain girl glares back at me: sullen brown eyes, smeared mascara, mousy hair. An entirely forgettable face. But for a couple of short years, I was someone's first thought in the morning, their first call, their last kiss goodnight. Now I'm discarded, dumped, and deleted; nothing but a dull memory, a buried piece of the past.

I'm going to teach you exactly what you taught me, Rena: Life is unfathomably cruel.

I'll never forget how it started. October twenty-fifth, a Halloween party approaching. A torn-out sheet of spiral-bound paper, folded neatly and slipped into my locker. My heart somersaulted as I discovered it. I unfolded it and trembled as I read the words.

Dear Jalyn

I've been watching you. I'm sorry, lol—that sounded creepy. Don't worry...I'm not a stalker. I just like to look at you in Algebra. I think you're cute. I wish I had the guts to ask you out.

I immediately stuffed it in my jeans, my cheeks six shades of scarlet, watching every passing face, wondering which classmate had contrived this awful prank. Every circle of conversation seemed like a private ambush. Every laugh floated in my direction. But no one stepped forward to shove a camera in my face.

I studied the note for a week—clearly the source of someone's secret amusement—knowing it couldn't be real. Praying I was wrong.

And then I received the second note.

Dear Jalyn

I'm going to text you this week. Don't freak out!

The handwriting was neat and deliberate, as if someone had taken great pains to write it. I imagined the person going through multiple drafts to craft just the right version for me.

Me!

Before those notes, the most attention I'd received was a muttered apology over a closed door slammed in my face.

For days, the notes never left my pocket. Like an addict, I stole glances everywhere: in the bathroom, in the locker room, in my car. I fantasized about who wrote the words. Was it a handsome stranger? A person I'd passed in the hallway once? A person I'd never expected? I became a shut-in, leaving my bedroom only for meals, to the utter dismay of my parents. But I wasn't depressed. I was thrilled. Sparks ignited my steps. I told no one, afraid that my secret might combust.

I waited a whole week to receive the promised text. When it came, I bolted upright, knocking my phone off the bed.

Hey Jalyn, it's me. From the notes.

Heart slamming against my ribcage, I replied: *Hey. Who's this?*

Lincoln.

???

Lincoln from Algebra.

I smiled through my quiet panic. My mind spun like a roulette wheel, waiting for something to slot into place. A name surfaced: *Lincoln Payne.* The new kid from Pennsylvania. We'd never spoken or even shared a glance that I remembered. My eyes drifted from the screen to the ceiling, recalling the quiet, dark-haired kid in the back of the room. I'd hardly noticed him. But now that I thought about him, I couldn't deny a building realization: he was cute.

I'll never forget our first conversation. Lincoln stood sideways by my locker while we talked, too nervous to face me, but his deep brown eyes drew me in, inviting me to stay longer. I called him "Mr. Stalker," breaking the tension, and he chuckled. His lopsided smirk made me want to say something funny right afterward—anything to stretch it wider. He was an introvert who liked long hikes and Shakespeare and quiet coffee shops. I was a soft-spoken rebel who pressed flowers in notebooks, listened to sad movie soundtracks, and left anonymous poetry on bathroom walls. Ours was an innocent love, two outcasts finding strength through our shared insecurity.

Our talks and phone calls continued; our feelings blossomed. Soon, I looked forward to his every smirk because they felt like mine and mine alone.

School was no longer a place I dreaded because Lincoln was there. I don't think I've ever enjoyed math class so much. It wasn't long before we were holding hands, exchanging shy hugs, playfully socking one another.

It took him a month to kiss me.

The wait was exciting. Torturous.

We sat on my bed, supposedly studying, Billie Eilish humming sullenly in the background. Sliding away our books, he sat close, knees barely brushing mine, and stared into my eyes. Then he leaned in—awkward and unsure, his breath warm, his hands trembling. He hesitated, lips parted. I didn't wait. I closed the space between us, kissing him first. It was clumsy and beautiful. I swear our souls collided that day. The world could've caved around us and we wouldn't have cared.

Lincoln was my life.

I stopped listening to my parent's lectures. I got a D in Algebra. Life was so much more than a GPA. Couldn't they see that?

We went to the Banshee, the arthouse theater, every weekend, watching indie films with quirky characters and plots we barely understood. We skipped school, spending weekends at the beach or sneaking into private pools until the police sent us scrambling. Once, Lincoln caught himself on a fence while escaping, losing a piece of his swimsuit and flashing the entire neighborhood.

I don't think I'd ever laughed so hard, or so uncontrollably.

We talked about places we'd been and places we hoped to travel, his childhood in rural Pennsylvania, and my small and quaint upbringing in Connecticut. He told me about the mist that curled above the Delaware

River and the covered bridges that creaked when you crossed them. He promised he'd take me there one day.

He even gave me a plastic ring from the Happy Tyme Arcade, blushing when he said he'd get me a real one day. And I believed him, because a fool always loves blindly.

You came into our lives the same way, like a drug I didn't know I needed. Somehow, Lincoln and I were accepted to Tunxis Community College, making a half-hearted attempt to build a future. Our parents had all but disowned us. I took a job washing dishes at Cherry Brook Nursing Home; he worked as a barista at Rebel Dog Coffee. We rented a studio apartment, barely making it, loving every minute.

For a while, we thought we knew better than everyone around us.

In reality, we didn't care, because we had each other.

He needed one more elective that semester, and we combed the coursebook, trying to find one that felt right. I immediately perked up when I saw *Introduction to Theater Arts*. He turned beet red and said he belonged in the audience, not on stage, but I assured him he'd do great—he'd memorized half the plays already; why not be in one?

Unsure of himself, he did his best Shakespeare-in-the-park impression.

I laughed as my breath caught; he was a natural.

Had I not been working at the nursing home, I would've enrolled with him. But too many shifts collided. I couldn't commit.

Lincoln soared in rehearsals, delivering incredible monologues that wowed even the professor. He earned the adulation of all his peers, receiving standing ovations on the regular. On a rare day off, I watched him audition for Puck in *A Midsummer Night's Dream*. He nailed it. It was no surprise that he landed the role.

I've never been prouder. Lincoln was brilliant. I was in love with an artist; a genius. Things were going great.

And you were about to take it all away.

You approached me in the auditorium, asking if the seat next to me was taken, introducing yourself as Titania. You laughed, before admitting your name was Rena. Although you were in the play, you liked to watch the rest of the cast when you weren't on stage. Your magnetism immediately disarmed me. You sat and I instantly blushed, gushing compliments. I marveled at your long, perfect hair and your polished style, noticing the way every head around you shifted toward you.

If I hadn't been so naïve, I might've detected the flash of envy on your face when I told you I was Lincoln's girlfriend. But you hid it well, Rena, like you hid the rest of your horrid sabotage. Every rehearsal I attended, you sought me out, spectating alongside me.

You knew exactly what to say to me. You complimented the braid in my hair, the way I coordinated my thrifted jackets, the way I spoke. Mellow and sweet. When I mentioned my job at the nursing home, you said I had the soul of a healer and that I should be a nurse. I laughed and shrugged it off. I was just a dishwasher; I didn't have a clear path. Psychologist? Maybe. Social worker? Possibly. What I didn't say aloud was that my one true calling was Lincoln.

I started seeing you around campus more and more, at the Happy Tyme Arcade, at the Commons, eventually at Rebel Dog Coffee. At first, the meetings were coincidental. You were always arm-in-arm with another guy—a classmate, an older man, all of whom lusted after you. They were your subjects and you, their queen. They would've risked everything just for a taste of your lips. Any inklings of alarm I had were smoothed over with a warm hug and an extra heap of praise for my hair. More than once, you linked your arm through mine, telling me I looked stunning, leaning in to whisper a private joke. Lincoln was a great actor, but you were the best, Rena.

You made me feel as if I could tell you anything.

And so I did.

I told you how Lincoln memorized his lines on our bed, how I played the rest of the cast, making up ridiculous voices. I admitted that I probably distracted him more than helped. I even told you how we made love one time while still in character. I immediately blushed, but you laughed away the awkwardness. You convinced me I was talented and that I should sign up the following semester. I sheepishly deflected.

To be fair, you're a talented girl, Rena.

You swept me into Shakespeare's world, too, selling me a story of unrequited love, dreams, and power. Your role as Titania made me think that magic was real.

But your true character—the one beneath—was cruel and twisted.

Winter wore into spring. The days melted into a barrage of run-throughs, line readings, and costume fittings. What began as scattered practice sessions became dress rehearsals—and then, just like that, it was here: opening night.

The play was billed for Thursday to Sunday; show after show, you and Lincoln captivated the enthusiastic attendees, igniting ripples of praise.

A trickle of curious theatergoers surged into a full house. When Sunday's matinee sold out, no one was surprised. I'd never heard such cheering as when you launched into your final monologue, Rena. You played Titania with venom and vulnerability. You held the audience in your palm, equal parts queen and wildfire. And Lincoln—God, Lincoln—he bounded across the stage like chaos incarnate, turning Puck into something more than comic relief. Brilliantly damaged.

You both deserved the As you earned in that class, and the standing ovation you received on closing night.

And when you cried during that final bow, I cried, too, not only for Lincoln, but for you. After the curtains rose, you stuck around until the three of us were alone, hugging as if we'd never let go.

Eventually, we disentangled, and you dabbed the makeup from your face.

Lincoln suggested that we have a quiet meal at the Olympia diner instead of the party everyone else left to attend. It felt wrong to leave you behind.

I might as well have invited you to dine on my still beating heart.

The next few months were so enchanting that I hardly realized the subtle changes. A hug where a kiss had once been. The slack feel of a hand, when only one person squeezes. The long silences when Lincoln and I were alone. We became an inseparable trio, wringing the life out of that sweltering summer. Lincoln and I took you to the Banshee, to the beach. We watched more movies than I can remember, cannonballing into private pools until our skins were pruned and our lips were blue.

You tried peppermint mocha at the coffee shop, admitting it wasn't as bad as you thought.

We passed the same cup between us.

We visited Happy Tyme Arcade, and Lincoln won another plastic ring—neon pink and far too big for my tiny fingers. With a theatrical bow, I turned to you, cradled it like a crown jewel, and dropped to one knee. We laughed until our sides split.

We hiked for miles at Heublein Tower and Castle Craig, swatting the bugs and admiring the views, rediscovering it all through your fresh eyes. In July, Lincoln scored tickets to a Broadway production of *Hamlet*, and we all went together to the city, critically nitpicking the players.

I humbly submitted that the pair of you were better performers; a pair indeed.

The first leaves of autumn were crisping and curling when you pitched an idea: It was almost the end of summer; why not visit Lincoln's hometown?

Lincoln and I glanced at each other. The trip to New Hope, Pennsylvania was supposed to be our big trip together; we'd just never found the time. He weighed it for a moment, but it wasn't a choice. Not really. With an enthusiastic smile, he looked between the two of us and burst out, "That sounds awesome. Let's do it!"

And so we set off in Lincoln's Subaru Crosstrek, just the three of us on the open road, blasting Led Zeppelin and Aerosmith, sharing stories of our relatives, forgotten heartbreaks, childhood hijinks. You told me about the time you and your best friend slept out in a tent in your parent's backyard, smoking your Dad's cigars, drinking warm beer. The image of twelve-year-old you and your redheaded friend puffing stogies cracked me up. Lincoln told us how he'd thrown a stink bomb during a middle school food fight, causing the ornery aide (and several sixth-grade girls) to vomit. We both nearly puked at the thought of it. I told you how I'd stolen tomatoes from my mother's garden, whipping them at the neighborhood bully, ending her fourth-grade reign of terror and earning myself a week's grounding. You told me how brave that was.

We ate at a Waffle House and immediately regretted it before stopping at every truck stop from here to the border. I don't think I've ever eaten so many bad hot dogs or congealed nacho platters. Every time you walked into a room, you turned heads without trying, as if the world unfolded around you. And me? I was honored to walk by your side.

Lincoln grew more and more excited as we drove into town, pointing out the New Hope railroad station, the old brick ice cream shop where he rode his bike, and the Bucks County Playhouse, where he swore that he saw the best *Othello* ever. I don't think I'd ever seen his face light up so brightly.

And then we were there: Sugan Road.

The street that had molded him.

It felt like we'd journeyed across the earth. But we'd made it.

Lincoln slowed the car to a crawl, pointing out the pale blue rancher with the cracked driveway, a netless basketball hoop leaning a little to the left—just a bit more tilted than he recalled. He cringed at a maple tree he'd once fallen out of. He parked at the end of the cul-de-sac, leading us down a weedy path to a narrow creek where he waded barefoot in summer, catching minnows in nylon nets. He showed us the elementary school playground where he'd broken his arm on the monkey bars. It was all there—smaller than he remembered, but alive with his youthful footprint. His lopsided grin had never been wider.

And I was thrilled for him.

On the way home, we stopped at the Delaware River, skipping stones, marveling at the current, dipping our toes before you playfully pushed me in. The cool water melted away the sweat of summer. I didn't complain, even though I didn't have a change of clothes. Neither did Lincoln, when I sat on his lap with my wet dress.

And then it was dusk.

With his signature grin, Lincoln told us he had one more thing to show us.

The sun glowed golden as we reached the VanSant bridge. Lincoln parked at the entrance, and we waited anxiously for traffic to clear before sneaking inside. My heart soared as we passed beneath the wooden canopy, inhaling the scent of tar and old timber. All at once, I was back in high school, picturing the note in my locker, reliving the moment Lincoln and I met, and our first, unforgettable conversations. I nearly cried recalling his promise to bring me here. It was the most spectacular moment of my life.

You let out a whoop of excitement, spinning in circles, and I took Lincoln in my arms, surprising him with a kiss. I should've noticed the way he pulled away, or your pinched expression when I pressed my lips against his.

The small shifts became yawning gaps. Awkward silences. Vacant stares.

A call from Lincoln, telling me he needed to stay late at work.

Then another.

He avoided any outings, telling me he'd rather spend date nights at home. He was tired of peppermint mocha. And wasn't the arcade boring? We spent less time together, and he picked up more shifts, blaming our tuition. We started arguing. We *never* argued.

Lincoln wasn't himself anymore. Our trip to New Hope had transformed him into a stranger who flinched at my touch.

I craved our rebellious days at the pool and those long, sunny days at the beach. His smile. The days when he couldn't wait to hear about my day, my superficial conversations with the terminally ill patients, suggesting maybe I might have a future in nursing, after all.

I wondered how it all broke down. But I already knew.

It was you, Rena.

It had always been you.

The nurses keep the fentanyl patches in the medication carts. They're supposed to dull the agony of dying, and in the beginning, they hid my pain. They say if you put them over the veins on your wrists, they reach the bloodstream quicker. It's true. Those first few doses soothed my constant heartache. They made me forget about the times I followed you to the arthouse theater, your arm hooked around Lincoln's, how I watched you instead of the show, laughing in the same places I once had, reciting the same familiar lines along with him. They helped ease the agony when I saw you kissing him at the arcade.

And they numbed the raw ache of watching you two perform *Hamlet* during the Fall semester, making eyes during the final bow before making love in the dressing room.

I never should've spied on you; it was too much to bear.

I wanted to cut you both into a thousand pieces.

I guess you really were a good actress, Rena. You made me think I was really worth a damn. You made me think I was special, like you, instead of the ordinary, ugly thing I am.

They say the drug's addictive, and I don't need a nursing degree to confirm that. I'm wearing two fentanyl patches on each wrist now, and I must say, it's quite the effective painkiller—for one of us, at least. I'm sorry that I couldn't spare one for you, but it's for the best. I feel almost nothing as you squirm and scream at me through your gag, begging for me to untie you from the chair. But I've got plans for you, Rena, and the walls are thick, and your neighbors aren't home. I grip my knife—

—and I'm immediately hit with euphoria. The substance surges, and my eyes roll back in my head. I stagger through the vertigo, recalling my plan, forcing it all back into focus.

For weeks, I've played out every revenge scenario, wondering which would suit you best. In my bittersweet fantasies, I've pushed you from a tower, tied you to the tracks, poisoned your champagne as we reminisce, me and you, my forever best friend. But you know what? Death is too kind for you. Revenge means drawing it out, Rena. It's no good unless you feel all the pain you put me through.

For you to *be me*.

I don't feel the sharp blade when I slice the skin from my forehead to my chin, a centimeter at a time, peeling it away, removing my loathsome face. But you certainly feel the pain when I slice off yours, creating a mask I'll stitch on and wear. I'm very gentle with it, Rena, taking great care. I wonder if it will be good enough to fool Lincoln? I've been practicing my acting skills, and I think I might just be able to pull it off.

I heard there's an opening in the theater class next semester and they're doing *Othello*.

Skin is everything in that story, I've heard.

I just might audition.

Look What You Made Me Do

By V. Castro

Banishment. The word cut deep as four voices rose above the din of clashing conversations. Almost as deep as the betrayal that led to this twisted justice. With dark clouds overhead I hoped it would rain on everyone gathered in the center of our village, where the coven was established two centuries before. I glanced towards Seraphina, my accuser, whose voice could be heard over the others, the howl of an evil spirit searching for a soul to consume and satiate its depravity.

Her eyes had a debauched look as she glared at me. Her heavy eyelids, smeared with black grease accentuated red tinged eyes. It was the intoxication of power. I could feel her hatred like ten poison-tipped flint arrows shot deep into my body and broken off with no way to pull them out. Her venom permeated the air.

"She wants all of you dead! At night she entices the men of the swamp to lay with her and exchange magic. She would use their sorcery against us! We must rid ourselves of her."

I was trapped within the stocks for three days, staring at a patch of grass yellowed from absorbing years of pooled vomit. My body trembled from hunger and thirst. She walked to the rusty lock with the key. In the other hand she held a water skin. My parched mouth yearned for a drop. She brought it close to my lips, fooling my glands into believing she would, but she didn't. She emptied the water skin and smiled as the hope drained from my face.

"Look what you made me do," she said with a wicked sneer that made her lips thin and curl to the shape of a serpent.

If I had any energy or spit in my mouth, I would have flung it at her. She unlocked the stocks, with the help of two sycophants who worshipped her like a goddess, lifted the top. They were fledglings, eager to ascend in the coven. Slowly, I stood upright. I groaned as the tension in the muscles in the back of my legs as tight as bow strings eased. My back spasmed as the weight of my torso created a series of hard, rock-like knots around my spine. The ache flooded all my senses. The skin around my wrists and neck burned. I had no choice but to soil myself when they first locked me in and I could smell that too. She chose humiliation before banishment to strip me of my dignity. But some things no one can take away.

I shook my head as I glanced around the gathered coven unwilling to look me in the eye. There was no *real* evidence presented that I had committed any of the crimes claimed by Seraphina. And the men of the swamp were less dangerous than her cries for purity, or those she kept close like armor. They roved through the abbey listening and watching for her. Little wicked spies. My body and my magic were my own. If I took a man from the swamp as a lover, it was no one's business. But fear is a useful whip to keep people pliable and docile. We were the two witches in our coven named by the High Priestess to take her place before she passed away. The next new moon one of us would be chosen as we would temporarily be possessed by her spirit.

Seraphina nodded at me. "We cannot have your impurities here. Go to the swamp where you belong. Your stench will hardly be noticed there."

I choked down a scream to defend my honor. But the seeds of doubt were planted in fertile soil, the villagers more ready to believe I was a witch than they were being misled. The beauty in witchcraft is there is always a way. As long as there was breath in my lungs, I would find it. I would speak the incantation with my final gasp.

To clear my name from Seraphina's sabotage, I would expose the liars. But I couldn't do it alone, or as I stood before the coven inches from death. As I turned to walk towards my quarters behind the village square, Seraphina rushed in front of me and blocked my way.

"No. She must not have anything with her. Into the wilds with nothing. As we feast you will starve. Go sell your body to the swamp men. Your filth is why you will never deserve to be High Priestess."

Her soulless black eyes burned like hidden embers. Dark pits of self-loathing and despair like the smoke that stained the beams of the grand hall behind her. Centuries of it layered in a thick tar. She hated to be challenged and that is why I found myself on the receiving end of her forked tongue. "Then why was I named?"

Her eyes narrowed. "The old woman valued your magic but she didn't know you were a whore."

Onlookers dodged my gaze in silence. None wanted to experience my fate. None trusted me and now I had lost all trust in them. But this wasn't over. Far from it. I didn't need the swamp men, although they did possess powerful magic. No, I sought succor from a darker place.

Seraphina raised her arm and pointed to the wide wooden gate in the center of the stone wall. The sooner I reached the forest the sooner I could enact my plan.

Alone with the clothes on my back and nothing else, I left the stone-walled village of my birth, hobbled my leaden limbs past the barley and wildflower fields and into the forest.

Near the border of the wood ran a creek. I kneeled in the mud and lapped up the water. The cold liquid filled my belly as my thirst grew. It ached from being empty for so long, but I had to drink. Some of my energy returned as the fog in my mind from dehydration cleared. The ache in my muscles eased and I felt I could walk faster now, with the haste befitting my plan.

The fresh spring water cleared the stale taste in my mouth. I had the urge to peel off my clothing. My trousers, crusted with dried urine, clung to my skin. The armpits and collar of my loose blouse were sweat-damp for three days. The only item of clothing that didn't feel uncomfortable was the shawl around my shoulders and apron around my waist.

I rose to my feet and ventured deeper into the forest hoping to encounter the only goddess I knew who could manifest the justice and chaos I sought. The edge of the wood became a spongy carpet of fallen, decaying leaves and thick green moss. The smell of the earthy dampness filled my nostrils. I walked with my eyes towards the ground looking for the dark beauty named Belladonna. The violet flowers were unique and wouldn't be difficult to discern within the foliage. However, it wasn't the flower I wanted. The dusky purple berries would deliver me to her. In death, I could have my life back. In death, I would become a nightmare my accusers would not see coming.

In death, I would call to Hel. I would offer her my life.

The deeper into the forest I walked the longer the shadows grew. Crows flew overhead, disturbed by my quick movements. I preferred the sound of flapping wings to that of lips. A sense of calm overtook me. Whatever happened, I had done my best.

I scanned the dark silhouettes of vegetation and finally saw a glint of moonlight reflected off that beautiful, poisonous skin. The berries are so lethal I only plucked three and placed them in the pocket of my apron. There was also still time to find a second suitable offering. Hares were abundant. We set traps for them at the edge of the field. This forest was generous to our village.

It was almost dusk, perfect timing as the rabbits would soon leave their burrows. I searched fallen trees for evidence of their presence. This time I walked slower, my steps as silent as a rabbit with the scent of a fox in its lungs. I took the wool shawl from around my shoulders and held it with both hands. In the distance, I saw a felled tree with a vast, intact network of branches. Closer, I found a hole dug out near the open end of a hollow tree. I stopped. A young hare stretched its limbs among the boughs. Now was my chance. I crept closer. The muffled snap of a twig alerted the rabbit, and it leapt out. Before it escaped, I tossed my shawl over it, sending it twisting and turning. I pounced and unsheathed my knife made from bear bone and flint. I pierced the shawl and into the rabbit's writhing body. One wound stilled its thrashing limbs.

I grasped its neck and gave it a hard twist to end the suffering. My fingers were slick with blood seeping through the shawl. I removed it and gave the head of the rabbit a light kiss.

"Thank you. You shall be a most potent offering," I whispered in its ear.

Now she had to be prepared. I slit open the hare from neck to tail and placed it on the tree. Blood and entrails spilled from its body. With one fingertip I touched this sacred sacrifice and drew Hel's rune sigil upon my chest. The warm blood on my skin was quickly chilled by the cool air of the forest.

I lay on the wet earth and placed the three Belladonna berries into my mouth. They burst with an acrid fluid coating my tongue and throat. I fought instinct to spit them out and swallowed. I was prepared to die. The cold of the ground crawled over my body like hungry leeches. My skin broke out into gooseflesh. Tree branches swayed overhead, leaves like dancing fairies. I held tightly to the wooden rune with Hel's symbol.

"I call to you my dearest wrath. Come to me great goddess of decay and beauty."

Tears slipped from the corner of my eyes recalling the humiliation of the stocks, the stench of sun-cooked vomit. My heavy eyelids lowered as darkness caressed them to a deep slumber.

"Hel," I croaked as my life ebbed from my body. The thrum of my heart slowed with every beat. An invigorated chill made the tips of my toes and fingertips tingle before a numbness encased me like a cocoon. I released my grip on the world, the invisible rope anchoring me to everything I'd known.

Hel would hear me.

My eyes were sealed shut, my awareness of them eroded when I felt something wet on my lips. I summoned the strength to open them again. One red eye met mine. The other was missing from an eye socket throbbing with maggots pulsing in the sticky red tissue. Chunks of fat and decayed flesh partially covered the exposed bone on half of her face. The other half glowed with a flawless complexion, thick eyelashes, and pink lips. She smelled of rot and spring. Light brown hair on half of her skull cascaded like a silty waterfall to my chest. Stringy wet strands clotted the other side.

She touched my belly with a decomposed, bony hand. I turned to my side and vomited. The undigested residue of the poison berries intermingled with mucus and bile.

"Thank you for offering your life and the life of the other. I found them both pleasing so here I am," she said.

I turned to her and wiped my mouth.

"You heard me. I am so grateful."

"Yes, death is my domain. Why did you pursue it to reach me?"

I sat upright against the tree. "Because I have been banished for something I did not do. I was humiliated at the Autumn Feast. My accuser is a liar and wants the world for herself, clean and pure. She hates those who dwell near the swamps, especially the men. She would have the coven live as forbidden fruit not to be touched. If she becomes High Priestess, I fear the wrath and destruction she could bring."

She touched my leg with her living hand. The wolf fur around the neck of her cloak rustled in the breeze.

"Others sought to bring you death in life. Destroy you without harming your body."

"Yes."

"And what would you ask of me?" Her red eye glowed brighter in the waning light.

"Help me to restore justice."

"What is the name of the accuser?"

"Seraphina."

She whipped her head in the direction of the village as if the trees were not there. "I know that name."

"How?"

"She called upon me to bring harm to others. She did not want justice but anguish with a spiteful heart. And she offered nothing."

Hel grabbed the dead hare by the ears. "With the blood of your offering I want you to write all the names who have aggrieved you. But make your mark beneath the one who caused you the most pain."

I inserted my fingers into the open torso, cracked the sternum and ripped the heart out, placing it on the dirt to use as an inkwell. With my bloody hand I began to make a list. Seraphina was at the top. With my knife I cut off one of the hare's legs. Beneath her name I dripped the blood into a line. Hel's stoic lips formed a tender smile. Then I used the inkwell bloody heart to write three more names.

"What must I do now?" I asked.

"Three nights. You will stay here for three nights. On the fourth night you will return to the village. At the darkest hour of the night, she will be revisited by her deeds. She will remember every word, lie, sensation of what she has done to you. She will see nothing but your face and feel all that you have experienced."

Warmth blossomed deep in my chest like roots seeking a water table. Tears fell like hot pearls. Hel made me feel like I didn't have to fight this battle alone. The smallness I felt in the stocks dissipated. "Thank you. I am humbled by your help."

"And that is why I offer my assistance. I will reveal myself when you face your accuser again."

Hel stood and unlatched her cloak. "It will be cold tonight. Wear this every night when you sleep and when you enter the village on the fourth night to confront Seraphina."

I took it from her. The fabric was soft. It smelled like burning leaves and menstrual blood.

"Thank you."

She nodded and walked towards the blackest part of the forest. Her form melted into the trees. Her feet became the soil. Her arms and legs could have been branches, or large ferns. Her hair the darkness in between the spaces of the material world and the unseen. My belly ached from vomiting, and I knew I needed real food. I looked at the dead hare I offered Hel. That could not be eaten, but there were many I could hunt.

I caught another rabbit, skinned it, and roasted it over a small fire. I was at peace in the darkness of the forest, curled up on my shawl with dried rabbit blood on my hands and face like a second skin. I covered my body with Hel's cloak. The wolf fur felt warm and comforting like the lighting of the hearth for the first time. It heats the soul and home. My eyes closed with the sound of the trees swaying in the air lulling me to a slumber. The leaves played their own symphony in the breeze. The forest after sunset is a place of nocturnal song. A hymn for what people fear. It felt like home. As I drifted, a part of me peeled away and wandered.

It was too real to be a dream. Unrooted. This had never happened before, but Hel said Seraphina would experience torment of her deeds as she slept. I released control of my mind and allowed it to fade into the night with lightness of a ghost. I had another body inside of me, one that unzipped my skin, desperate to escape. Over the trees, the wildflowers, the cold creek I flew into oblivion.

And then I awoke to the sounds of birds chirping overhead. The gloom of the previous day became sunlight falling on my face. I took it as a good omen. I closed my eyes and recalled the High Priestess touching my cheek as she named me as a possible successor. Sunlight had filled the room. The sky had opened as if a path for her spirit had been made. We'd held each other's gaze, and I saw she had no fear of death. She'd felt peace and I was happy for her. It was a good memory.

The last thing I remembered was floating away from my body and nothing after. Hunger rumbled in my belly. I glanced around hoping for something edible within reach. The hare carcass lay on the ground picked clean. Only the bones and fur remained. Next to my feet a fallen branch with a sharp edge pointed in the direction of the stream. My mouth salivated with the thought of a charred fat trout.

Two more days until I returned to the village. Hel didn't share all the details. I would have to wait and see. I'd spend my time hunting and resting, strip naked and wash in the stream. I'd cleanse the filth of shame off me. The shame others tried to impose. I'd use a smooth stone to scrub away the glares, judgment, and condemnation. Barbed words would be plucked from my mind before they festered into something worse. Water is a precious gift.

I walked towards the village and a bonfire at its center. Voices, music, and laughter filled the night. The iron-heavy aroma of cooking venison and the salty tang of baking bread revived my hunger. Rabbits staved off starvation but the meat was lean and unsatisfying. The thought of warm bread with thick slabs of butter made my mouth water. I would have it this night.

Seraphina stood next to the bonfire wearing the crown of antlers and shattered skulls of our dead elders. She didn't earn this right. She took it with lies and coercion. Three of her lackeys stood next to her filling her cup with wine, fiddling with her hair, or whispering in her ear. They giggled like children and pointed to the villagers as if suggesting the next target.

I approached her as Hel instructed. The music stopped, and the rowdy noise of the crowd turned to hushed whispers. My hair was braided with ivy and hare bone. My clothing was beyond salvaging, so all I wore was Hel's cloak. My body was on display without shame or fear. And I knew my nakedness would enrage Seraphina. Her eyes widened, reflecting bonfire flames when she saw me. Perhaps she would burn from the inside out.

"You vile sorceress! You have been in my dreams! You have tried to kill me! I told you she dealt in swamp magic! She dares show herself nude? A true whore of the swamp stands before us." She looked deranged as she shouted. Spit flew from her twisted mouth. The black grease around her eyes was smeared in such a way to make her eyes look like empty sockets. The rest of her skin glistened from the calf fat she used to keep herself looking young.

"*I* am not of the swamp and the power I wield is greater than your understanding!" A voice boomed across the field.

The crowd gasped as Hel approached Seraphina. The black gown plunged to her navel exposing half a ribcage with a black beating heart inside and a perfectly formed breast with a taught pink nipple. Her skin sparkled with dew in the firelight. On her head was a crown made from gold and teeth. In the center a bright oval shaped clear crystal caught the color of the bonfire.

Seraphina threw herself at the feet of the goddess.

"I beg you to take mercy."

Hel stood over her. Maggots writhed free of her empty eye socket. The thick flab of rotten muscle stretched across her jaw tightened as she spoke.

"Oh, my dear. How you cry for yourself so that others will cry for you too. However, the unseen sees all! You have harmed a loyal daughter. She offered her life to me, the greatest of offerings."

Seraphina bowed her head. "I did not know. Show me mercy, beautiful Hel. I too want to be your daughter. Tell me what to do. I will burn entire villages in your name. We will sacrifice the people who dwell in the swamp for you."

"Mercy? Death knows no such thing. Death is neither kind nor evil. It is part of all that moves in the heavens and here in your world. And slaughter is not an offering."

Seraphina raised her eyes towards the goddess and scowled as she rose to her feet.

"There are deities more powerful than you and I have their favor. You do not scare me."

"Is that what you think?" Hel gently kicked dirt in Seraphina's direction. The dust flew into the air and landed upon Seraphina in the form of spiders, centipedes with large pinchers, and earthworms.

"You vile and wicked creature!" shrieked Seraphina, limbs shuddering to cast off the bugs.

Hel laughed. "How quickly your loyalty slips when you don't get what you want. And, you should fear me."

Hel faced the crowd and pointed her human hand at the flames. "Look and see!"

From the bonfire came the voices of Seraphina and her cohorts. Conversations of people they wanted to banish. A plan to conquer villages from there to the swamp.

"Swamp sorcery!" screamed Seraphina.

"The only lies come from you," I said loud enough for everyone to hear.

One of her spies moved towards Hel. "It is true. All of it. I was part of it. Hel does not lie."

She turned to me. "I am sorry. But I was afraid."

"I know. I know all of you are."

"I will kill you!" Seraphina lunged towards me.

Hel grasped Seraphina with her dead hand and tossed her to the ground. The coven scuttled away as her body skidded into the stocks where she imprisoned me for three days. The snap of cracking wood made me smile. The crown of bones fell from her head. Hel stomped towards the crumpled woman, her black gown like nightfall. Seraphina attempted to rise to meet her. She plucked a shard of bone from her crown and hurtled it at the goddess.

"You believe you matter, but in death we are all nothing. Now you will experience it."

Hel grabbed Seraphina by the wrist, digging the tips of her bony hand into her forearm. Blood bubbled from the punctures. Hel dragged her away from the stocks, her tight grasp leaving Seraphina unable to move.

Hel looked to me. "Any last words before I take her?"

I knelt before my adversary. I could smell the stench of sweat and fear coming from the tuft of hair in her armpit. In her ear I whispered, "There will never be a next time for you but maybe don't be such a deplorable cunt. Look what you made me do."

I glanced towards Hel and nodded. "A third offering, great goddess. I am always at your disposal and on this day every year I shall have a great feast in your honor."

Hel smiled at me. Her red eye glowed brighter. I knew she found this pleasing. She turned and dragged a screaming Seraphina by the wrist. The sound didn't stop until they reached the forest.

Shake It Off

By Red Lagoe

"Renata, where's all your stuff?" my new friend, Aimee, asked as she stepped into the trailer home.

"We lost everything in the fire."

I closed the door, adjusting my backpack, which was barren of charm and personality, unlike Aimee's.

Her backpack was adorned with colorful buttons and patches as loud as her personality. She was a fellow junior classmate with mile-high hair sprayed into a poof. As the new kid, I wasn't well-acquainted, but I knew she had a boyfriend who wasn't nearly as friendly as she.

"Mom moved us in two weeks ago, but I don't really remember it."

Aimee's eyes lit with eager curiosity. "So, it's true!"

"What?"

"Do you really have amnesia?"

"Where'd you hear that?"

"That's what people say." Aimee moved across the living room's hunter green carpet toward the kitchen. Mom had yet to replace all the furniture we'd lost in the old house. A second-hand loveseat with floral cushions faced a wall with no television.

"My memory will come back."

"So, you don't remember *anything*? Did you wake up and say, 'what year is it?' And someone told you it's 1989?" She gasped and feigned disgust. "Wake me up in the 90s, will ya?"

"Something like that," I said.

"Where'd you move from?"

I shrugged. "All I remember is bandages."

"From burns? Do you have scars?"

"I don't think so."

"How is that possible?" Aimee opened the kitchen cabinets to reveal paper plates and Styrofoam cups. She ran her fingers along empty counters, the folding card table, and chairs. Then she set her attention down the hallway of blank walls.

My lower lid twitched with a muscle spasm.

"How does a fire make you lose your memory?"

She meandered toward the bedrooms.

"Not sure."

I scratched my buzzcut head and followed her.

"Didn't you ask?"

Her incessant questioning skittered under my skin like a thousand bugs. I wanted to crawl into my bed and hide because I should've known the answers.

"I was kind of out of it after I woke up."

Aimee tested the knob on my mother's bedroom door, but it was locked.

"She doesn't want anyone in there when she's not home," I said.

"Weird."

She moved on to my bedroom, where a twin mattress sat on the floor. Boxes were stacked on their sides with flaps folded in as makeshift cubbies for clothes.

Aimee peeked out my window into the backyard. "All these trailers have the exact same layout. This room is where my bedroom is, too. I'm number five, three trailers down."

The Polaroid on top of my boxes grabbed her attention next, and she studied the image of my mother and me.

"That was taken last week," I said.

"Do you have any pictures from before the fire?"

"They all burned."

Aimee's hand went to her heart. "Maybe some relatives have pictures."

I shrugged, skin itching in response to her prying observations.

"What about your dad? Where's he?"

"I don't know!" I snapped. I caught my reflection in the small plastic-framed mirror on the wall. Buzzed blonde hair, square jaw, straight eyebrows, and ice-blue eyes. I'd stared at that face for days after waking, but my reflection remained a stranger.

"Renata." Her eyes bore holes into me like curious daggers trying to carve out information. "Something is off here."

The front door creaked open, and keys jingled.

"That's my mom."

Aimee hurried down the hall where my mother stood in her light blue nurse's uniform. Her E.R. badge hung from a lanyard around her neck. Of all the things I couldn't remember, at least my mother seemed familiar. Her wild, red hair was loosely pulled back in a bun. A cigarette hung from her lips, and sunlight from the window lit up its tendril of smoke. She locked eyes with me as she set her things on the couch. A nervous trembling rattled through my legs, and I had to flex my muscles to stop it.

"Hi! I'm Aimee." She extended a hand.

Mom accepted Aimee's handshake, but kept an eye on me. "Elaine Vincent." A grin stretched across her face, crow's feet deepening, but her smile was strained. "I'm so glad Renata is making friends."

Aimee tilted her head. "Sorry about what happened to you guys."

Mom took a puff from her cigarette and exhaled. "What's important is that he's alive." She came to my side and wrapped an arm around my shoulder.

"So, you're a nurse?"

Mom released me and studied her cigarette as the cherry reached the filter. "I am."

"Aren't people with amnesia supposed to stay where it's familiar? Why'd you move away?"

"That's none of your business, young lady."

"Mom ..."

Aimee's hands went up in surrender. "I'm just trying to help."

Mom stood taller, as if trying to take up more space. "If you want to help, you can leave."

"Mom!" My heart raced with embarrassment, and I chewed on my bottom lip so hard I thought it might tear away from my face.

Mom's eyes softened. "Pardon my manners. I appreciate your concern, Aimee, but Renata is still recovering and needs his rest."

Aimee furrowed her brow. "Yeah, okay. See you at school."

Mom extinguished her cigarette in the ashtray on the card table, and I followed Aimee outside.

"Sorry about that. I guess she's protective," I said, closing the door.

"Yeah, of her secrets! That was weird, dude."

I dragged my fingernails along my irritable skin. "Is it?"

"Yes! That woman is up to something. Do you have proof there was a fire? Was it in the newspaper?"

"I don't know."

"Is there a record of your hospital stay?"

The pressure of each piling question weighed so heavy, I thought I could collapse.

"You look nothing like her."

"What are you getting at?"

"Don't you watch America's Most Wanted?" she said.

"I–" I couldn't remember.

"I don't think that woman is your mother."

I twirled spaghetti around my plastic fork not recalling having ever done it before. I couldn't remember learning geometry, yet I knew the material in class. I could tie my shoes, speak, all without remembering how.

"How do I know to twirl it?"

"Muscle memory," my mother said. Her face was pallid, eyes sunken and tired. Was this the face I'd seen when I was born? The face of the woman who raised me?

"Mom..." The word lingered on my tongue, souring the flavor of spaghetti sauce. "I didn't ask before, but I think I'm ready to know more about my life. Like, where did we live?"

Her fork punctured the paper plate, but she did not lift her eyes. "New York. We couldn't afford it with the medical bills from your injuries. That's why we had to move."

"What about family?"

"It's just you and me. Always has been."

"Did I have a dad?"

Mom sighed, leaned back, and set her fork down. She studied me for a moment and smiled. "You're getting older. Where did my little boy go?"

"Do I look like him? My dad?"

Mom stared through me, as if lost in memory. Her lower eyelid twitched before she slowly turned her attention to the pack of Virginia Slims at the center of the table. "Not so much anymore."

"Where is he?"

She reached for her pack of cigarettes, pulled out a smoke and lit it. The stench of smoke and menthol filled the room. "Your father left when I was still pregnant with you. He changed his identity, and I haven't seen him since."

"Oh."

"You don't need a man like that in your life anyway."

"There was nobody else in our lives? I had friends, didn't I?"

She scooted her chair around the corner of the card table and reached for me. A squirming sensation in my gut warned me to get out from under her touch, but I didn't want to hurt her feelings as she placed her palm against my cheek.

She pulled back, took a drag from her cigarette, and tapped the ash into the metal lid from the marinara jar. "You were bullied at your last school. It made leaving easy."

"Bullied?"

"But I'll tell you something about yourself you don't know yet. You have this ability to …well, whenever life gets hard, whenever people are mean and insufferable, you can just shake it off like nothing ever happened. You are stoic and resilient, and *that* is a superpower."

The phone rang and Mom patted me on the head before she stood, turned, and lifted the beige receiver from the wall.

"Hello?" She stretched the curled cord between her fingers. "Yes ..."

There was a subtle shift of her spine from rigid to relaxed. A deep inhale and exhale. What was it about her that felt familiar? I stared as if I could force a memory to materialize in the five feet between us. The yellow halogen light glinted off the silver fly-aways in her red hair, and a vision came to me. She was driving with the windows rolled down. Her hair blew like a tangled nest of snakes. I smelled menthol cigarette smoke. Probably why the windows were down. She twisted to look at me as I roused in the back seat, peering through a gap in facial bandages.

"It'll be okay, sweet boy," she said then. "I'll be there shortly." Mom hung up the phone. "I got called in for the late shift. We'll talk about this more tomorrow, okay?"

I stayed at the card table while Mom tossed our paper plates into the trash. "Clean up the pans?"

I nodded, and Mom rushed around the house to grab her things, ensuring her Virginia Slims were packed and her bedroom door was closed. Then she was out the front door, carrying with her all the answers to my questions.

What was she hiding? Aimee was right. It was weird. Without memory, I had no basis on which to gauge something's weirdness, yet it still felt off. At the same time, core emotions and instinctual feelings were telling me that she was my mother, and that I could trust her. That had to mean something, right?

I went to bed that evening, restless with questions and suspicions. If Elaine Vincent was a woman I could trust, then why did her words feel like partial truths? After my bedside clock hit midnight, it was apparent that sleep would not come, so I paced the floors. There was no radio in the house yet, no television, nothing but a couple of magazines Mom brought home from work. I tried flipping through, hoping the celebrities would ring a bell, but nothing did. My fingers dragged along the empty hallway walls and across my mother's bedroom door. It pushed open, and I grabbed the knob. It was locked, but my mother must not have closed the door tightly in her hurry to leave.

I checked to be sure her station wagon was still gone before entering her bedroom. She had a full-sized bed with a metal frame. Her clothes were piled neatly in two suitcases on the floor. There was nothing on her walls, no art or knickknacks. No memories of our life together.

Behind a curtain, peeking underneath it, a shape was nearly lost in shadow. I crossed the room, neck hairs standing at attention and skin threatening to crawl off my body, as if she might materialize behind me. I swept the curtain aside to find a Polaroid of me in my new school clothes atop a cardboard box. I moved the picture and unfolded the cardboard flaps to reveal a baby blanket laying on top of a file box within.

The metal box inside was locked with a flimsy clasp. Certain my mother had the key on her, I didn't bother searching for it. I grabbed a hairpin from the medicine cabinet in the bathroom, peeked out the front window again, then rushed back to her room. I couldn't recall where I'd seen it done before, but my fingers worked clumsily at the lock until the mechanism released and the clasp broke open.

Inside, lay a document that was difficult to read in the darkness, but when I held it to the window, scant light from the moon revealed it to be a birth certificate from the state of Michigan for Renata Vincent. The mother was recorded as Elaine Vincent, and the father was David Walker.

David Walker, I repeated it several times, burning the name into my memory so I could look him up in public records. I set the birth certificate aside and rifled through old bank statements with addresses from Chicago to Syracuse to Birmingham.

A flash of a tall black building in a city skyline came to me. Then an on ramp for route 695. I closed my eyes and tried to let the memories return, but the harder I tried, the more elusive they became. So, I dug through the box until my fingers fell upon a thick, unsealed envelope full of photographs.

I brought the stack of pictures into the moonlight, but it wasn't enough to identify the faces, so I ran into the hallway where light from the bathroom across the hall allowed a more thorough examination. From there, I could still keep an eye on my mother's window to be sure she didn't return.

The first photograph was of young Elaine Vincent, unmistakable vibrant, curly hair, holding an infant with dark hair. On the back of the photograph, written in blue ink, was "1972", the year I was born. Why would she keep this baby picture hidden?

The next photo was of a toddler-aged child and Elaine in bell-bottoms, bent over with hands hooked under his armpits. This child had dark hair. No blonde had come through. He had full lips, a joker-grin smile, and dimples. A stark contrast to my thin lips. I reached for my cheeks, feeling for dimples, but they would not emerge even when I forced a smile. The baby aged with each new image. There was a young boy on a bike with the same curls and joker grin. Another of the boy in a Halloween costume, brown curly hair growing longer and unruly. He looked so much like Elaine Vincent, but absolutely nothing like me. The last photo of the boy with mousy brown curls was of him sitting before a birthday cake with the number eleven on top.

In the next photo, another boy took his place. His hair was straight and black, and his skin was translucently pale unlike the previous kid's olive undertones. There were three images of the pale kid before he was replaced by a young teenager with blonde hair and a pointy chin. And another, slightly older boy after that with buzzed brown hair and narrow eyes. Four different boys were in the photos with my mother while she gained new wrinkles and added grays.

A stress spasm under my skin tap-tap-tapped at my nerves and made me shiver.

I don't think that woman is your mother. Aimee's voice reverberated through my head, vibrating against my skull so hard the sensation of her words tingled in my scalp. I scratched at my stubbly hair and looked into Elaine's makeup mirror, tugging at the skin around my eyes trying to see if there was a resemblance to any of the boys in the photographs.

Was I the next boy who would disappear? If she kidnapped me, how? Drugs? Blunt force trauma? How did she wipe my memory? And what happened to those four other boys?

Headlights poured through the window, alerting me to the station wagon pulling in. I ducked out of view and scrambled to stack everything back into the box as I had found it. The vehicle door shut, and I folded the box flaps closed and placed the photo on top. The sound of keys in the front door jingled as I quietly closed Elaine Vincent's bedroom door. Two seconds later, the front door opened, as I threw the comforter over my body.

I faced the opposite wall as she stepped into my room. I felt her looming over me as if she held a gun or a can of gasoline, ready to move on to the next kid. I wanted to jump from bed and sprint into the woods, go get Aimee, and ask her to run away with me. I wanted to cry. I wanted to scream. I wanted to disappear. But all I could do was hide beneath my covers and lay perfectly still. Every cell in my body wanted nothing more than to vanish from her sight. My heart beat so fast I thought it might separate from my body, so I tried to keep my breathing shallow so Elaine Vincent wouldn't suspect anything.

My door clicked shut, and I twisted around to find I was alone. Only the smell of cigarette smoke remained. I knew few things for certain. But I understood Elaine was not to be trusted. I couldn't confront her and become a new addition to her photo collection. Instead, I threw some clothes into my backpack and unlatched the window. It screamed open, cutting through silence, and in my frantic attempt to escape, I clumsily caught my foot on the window screen. It crashed to the floor. I should have taken my time, moved with stealth, but panic took over, and instinct insisted that I run.

Before I made it across my yard, Elaine's bedroom light blazed on. Her silhouette appeared in the window. Without hesitation, I cut down the driveway through the trailer park. My legs were weak and tired like it was the first time I'd ever run, but I pushed through the spasming muscles toward Aimee's place. The white lattice fence around Aimee's yard provided cover as I ducked out of sight. I rounded the corner behind her trailer, and my foot caught on the frame of a tricycle, sending me crashing into the grass. Motion lights drenched me in a blinding glare, further calling attention to my presence, and Aimee's curtains flung open. Her hair spilled out of a ponytail. A cropped tee-shirt hung from one shoulder, and her mouth hung open in surprise to see me crouched outside her bedroom window. "Renata?"

Travis, Aimee's boyfriend, appeared beside her. "Is that the weird kid with no memory?"

"Shhh." She smacked him in the chest. "If my dad wakes up, we're dead."

I ducked as the sound of tires hissed and headlights passed by. "Can I come in?"

"Hell no!" Travis's voice raised above a whisper.

"Shh!" Aimee backhanded him in the chest again.

"You might be right about my mom." My stomach flipped upon saying it. I held my hand over my mouth, trying not to let my guts spew out.

"Are you serious?"

"You gotta help me."

Aimee checked over her shoulder. "I can't right now."

"I don't know what to do."

"Call the cops or something!" Aimee's eyes were wide with panic, and my reflection within them was frail and lost within her gaze.

She shook her head and as she closed the window with a cringe, she whispered, "I'm sorry!"

A dog next door barked, and I felt like a prisoner escaping a maximum-security institution. I took off toward the street, and had to duck behind the trash bins as Elaine Vincent's station wagon rolled by. I crouched, shaking so hard I thought I might explode. If only I could crawl into the trash bins and never be seen by my mother or Aimee or anyone ever again. My hands shook violently, and then the trembling extended up my arms, across my chest, and vibrated at my core. Anxiety coursed through me in waves of spasmodic fits as the station wagon rolled out of sight.

"Hey!" Travis called from behind.

I leapt up, running out of the trailer park and into the woods.

"What the hell are you doing at my girlfriend's house? She only talked to you to find out if you were lying about the amnesia."

"I'm sorry." I walked as fast as I could between the trees, tremors rattling my bones. My face drooped on the left side, and words failed to form. They dribbled out as illegible sounds, tongue and lips betraying me.

Travis seized my shoulder and forced me around. "What's wrong with you?"

He landed a glancing blow to my cheek. Upon impact skin ripped away and was flung through the moonlight, disappearing into the columns of tree shadows.

Travis' face contorted into shock, and he staggered backward.

I screamed with such ferocity that a shockwave erupted, rippling across my body. My ribs cracked into pieces, snapping louder than the branches beneath Travis' feet as he pushed through gnarled brush to get away from me. My skin cleaved open like patchwork over my arms, neck, and chest. It sloughed off of musculature, exposing the shifting pink flesh underneath. Bones crunched and distorted. Sharp searing pain ravaged my body as if mangled by a pack of lions. I tore at my clothes, and as the fabric peeled off, skin, muscle, and sinew stripped away with it. The air scalded my raw flesh with the agonizing intensity of a burning flame.

Travis's silhouette vanished at the edge of the woods. A streetlight between the trees became a beacon, and I staggered toward it as parts of my flesh dropped in a trail behind me. With each shiver and jolt, bits of myself fell away.

I staggered out of the trees, and bloody, wet meat glistened under the glow of the streetlamp. As a station wagon pulled up alongside me, my vision tunneled, and I dropped to the pavement.

"I've got you, my sweet boy," Elaine Vincent said.

Bandages laid across my skin. Elaine came in and out of focus as she tended my wounds. Each time I opened my eyes, her outfit was different, and daylight shifted across the walls.

She cried at my bedside. "I don't know how much you'll remember this time, but you should know that you've done this before. First, when you were eleven. You wet the bed at a sleepover, and you were so embarrassed that you wanted to disappear. Thank goodness, you ran home to ... *change*. You can't begin to imagine what I went through, seeing your body fall apart like that. I thought you were good as dead. So did the doctors. We didn't know what to think when the bandages came off, and there was a different boy. I was so angry with those doctors. We all thought there was some sort of mix up, but nobody could figure out where you went and where this other kid came from. But *I* figured it out. A mother can recognize her baby, even with a different face. I had to run away with you. Long story short, my sweet boy, you grew a new identity when life got too hard. Then again, a couple years later. And again, a year after that. But this time, it was only two weeks!"

She wiped tears from her eyes, and I slipped back into darkness.

Mom peeled a bandage from my arm to reveal healthy, pink flesh.

"It's healing. You'll be okay to travel soon. We're moving to Phoenix this time. How fitting."

I opened my eyes to a blue sky and the desert on the horizon. I was in the back of a station wagon, but couldn't remember why. In the driver's seat, I saw wild, red hair with silver glints of sunlight. The woman driving said, "You get it from your father. Some people would give anything to escape their lives and start anew. The ability to shake it off and start life with a whole new perspective ... that's a blessing, isn't it?"

I opened my eyes to stark white walls. Blackout curtains hung on the window. I jolted to attention, body aching as if I'd been hit by a truck. I slid my feet over the edge of the mattress that sat directly on the floor, and a middle-aged woman with curly red hair entered the room to calm my worries.

"Renata," she said it as a sigh, as if I was a balm to her ailing heart. "I'm your mom. There was an accident—a fire—and you were in a coma for a few weeks. They said your memory might be a bit foggy, but it'll come back. What's important is that you're safe. And we're together."

I looked at my freckled arms and rubbed the scruff on my sore jaw. It ached like someone had taken a wrench to my bones. The woman who called herself my mother sat beside me on the bed and gave me a handheld mirror. I had short auburn hair, a face full of freckles, and the eyes of a familiar frail and lost person who was tired of shaking in fear, and tired of the lies. But what lies?

The mother placed her hands on my face, and tears filled her eyes like she hadn't seen me in years. There was something familiar about her, aside from an odd sense of motherly love. As she leaned in for a hug, the stench of Virginia Slims wafted from her clothes. I pulled away as a flash of blood and broken bone blinked in my internal vision. A voice within warned that I couldn't hide any longer. It rippled through my body as a shiver and I felt myself harden to trauma I could not remember.

"What really happened?" I asked.

"Just like I said, my sweet boy. I think you need some rest."

There was a tap-tap-tap of a spasm under my skin and a rattle in my core insisting I shouldn't trust her, that I should run and hide, that I should shed my skin and disappear. But the scared kid in the mirror wasn't me anymore. No. This version of me would be unshakeable.

A sad smile crept onto her lips, and she studied me, eyes wide and worried. The woman backed toward the door, hand trembling on the knob. "It's gonna be all right."

Vigilante Shit

By Zach Bohannon

He pushed her against the wall because it felt exhilarating.

And Cameron Rainey loved holding power and control over others—*especially* women.

He grabbed a handful of her curly, red-streaked brown hair and pulled the woman's head back to look up at him. At six-foot-two, Cameron towered over her, which only turned him on more—his size, a reflection of his strength and masculinity. The woman (Tara...or was it Joanna?) gazed up at him, her dark makeup accentuating her bright green eyes, and her crimson lipstick smeared from his hard kiss. He gripped her toned, exposed stomach, and kissed her again.

The woman pushed against him, but Cameron kept her pinned to the stall. She could move when he allowed her to. To show that, he pushed her back hard against the stall, rocking it.

"What the fuck?" a woman called from the other side.

The fact that they were in the club's bathroom also turned him on. It felt dirty and wrong and hot. And he could get exactly what he wanted out of Whatever Her Name Was without having to leave the club.

"You like to be dominant, don't you?" she asked.

"Yes," he said, pressing his thumbs into her hips.

What's Her Name put her hand on his left cheek and slid her long, manicured nails down the side of his neck. "I like to be in control, too."

That turned Cameron off, but he went with it. "Oh, yeah?"

She nodded, then placed both hands firmly on his shoulders and pushed him against the other side of the stall. Cameron's back slammed against it; the move caught him by surprise and he laughed.

A light flicked above, long enough for him to get a good look at the woman standing across from him. Her nipple rings pressed through her white crop top, and her leather pants were low enough to expose her defined hips. No wonder he was in this dirty women's restroom with her.

She thrust forward, putting her hands on his chest and pressing herself against his manhood. Her hands slid up to his face again, and she stood on tiptoes to kiss him. Then, she moved to his cheek, licking her way to his ear. When she nibbled on his earlobe, she reached between his legs, finding him firm and ready.

Cameron moaned, closing his eyes.

He leaned his head back as she stroked him through his pants and moved from his ear to his neck. Her full lips kissed him twice, then she slid her tongue over a sensitive spot.

"Fuck, baby," he muttered. "That feels so goddamn—"

She bit his neck hard enough that Cameron's eyes shot open and he grabbed her by the shoulders. He threw her hard into the other side of the stall and raised his hand to his neck. Cameron felt warm blood on his fingers.

"What the fuck?" he yelled, narrowing his eyes.

"What?" Her lips parted. "I thought you'd like it rough."

"I don't want a goddamn scar, you fucking skank!"

He pulled his hand away from his neck to see blood on his fingertips. The bitch had bitten the shit out of him. Cameron's eyes drifted to the woman as she licked his blood from the corner of her mouth.

"You sick bitch."

He threw the stall door open, nearly hitting another woman who screamed out and jumped back. "Asshole!"

Ignoring her, Cameron stormed out of the women's restroom and went to the men's.

Cameron exited the men's room several minutes later, still irritated by what had happened. He'd sweated through his long-sleeve silk button-up but managed to freshen himself up and no longer had a swamp in his armpits.

That bitch better have left. I don't want to see her face again.

He walked down the hallway as the pulse of the electronic music grew louder, thumping in his chest. He needed a drink.

Cameron found an open seat at the end of the bar with four other empty seats around him, giving him some space. The bartender, a twenty-something guy with shaggy hair, probably working towards a worthless political science degree, came over.

"Old Fashioned," Cameron said.

The bartender nodded. For the kid's sake, Cameron hoped the drink was good, since he would be a bartender for years to come.

He brought the drink over and asked if Cameron wanted to start a tab. Cameron shook his head and handed the kid a thick black credit card.

The bartender took the card and moved it up and down in his hand, feeling the weight of it. He glanced at it, then back to Cameron, before whistling and strolling to the register. The kid had clearly never seen an elite status black card before. The sort of credit card companies only handed out to top tier customers.

"That's a hell of a hefty card," the bartender said, handing it back to Cameron. "And my machine didn't even think about it when I swiped it; it approved instantly."

Cameron nodded, shoved the card back into his gunmetal minimalist wallet, then took a sip of his drink. The kid had done alright. Plenty of whiskey and not too heavy on the bitters.

As he nursed the drink, Cameron glimpsed a beautiful woman over the rim of the glass. She sat alone at the other end of the bar wearing a form fitting purple dress with a plunging neckline. Dark hair rested on her shoulders and her face wasn't overly disguised with makeup. She couldn't have been any older than the bartender. Cameron preferred them that way—at least ten years younger. He was thirty-three.

They met eyes and she smiled, but he couldn't give in that easily. Cameron humored her for a moment before looking away. He reached into his pocket and retrieved his phone, hoping to seem disinterested enough that she would *really* want him.

His screen lit up, populated with several notifications in front of his background—a picture taken from his beach house in Outer Banks, North Carolina. The bright screen suddenly nauseated him. Cameron looked away, rubbing his eyes and his head. After a few moments, he tried looking at the screen again. He still felt a little weird but shrugged it off.

A few of the notifications were from social media apps. Another was from his crypto app. Then, he had text messages from his best friend

Joey, a boring bank teller named Christy who he'd hooked up with a few times—he swiped that one away without checking it—and one from a number not saved in his phone.

He tapped the last one.

Hey! It's Ruby. Do you remember me?

Ruby? Who the fuck was Ruby? Cameron searched his mind, trying to remember. His head throbbed, bringing on a headache that didn't help his efforts.

Yeah of course. How are you doing Ruby?

The dreaded dots danced across the screen. Her next text appeared.

I'm in town. Was hoping you might want to get together.

Cameron scoffed. He glanced at the woman at the end of the bar again. She was still looking at him. And he didn't even remember who the hell this Ruby chick was.

I don't know. I'm a little busy tonight.

He took another sip from his drink and finally smiled at the cute co-ed when his phone buzzed.

Aww that's a bummer. I had so much fun with you last time. We were really hoping you'd be available tonight to hang out.

Cameron raised an eyebrow. "We? What the hell did that mean?"

We? Are you in town seeing a friend?

More dots. He glanced up again. The girl waved at him this time, shyly. Cameron lifted the corner of his mouth and winked at her. Then, his phone buzzed again.

This time, it wasn't a text, but a picture.

His eyes went wide.

Three women squeezed into the photo, their breasts exposed. The picture only showed them from their necks to midway down their stomachs, not showing their faces. One tan, another fair-skinned, and the last with a milk chocolate tone. Each had large breasts, their nipples hard. Cameron instantly got hard himself.

More dots.

We've been having some fun by ourselves but it's getting kinda boring. I was really hoping you'd wanna see me again.

Cameron had never typed faster in his life.

Text me the address.

Stepping out of the ride-share vehicle, Cameron slammed the door. The driver rolled down his window.

"Damn, man. You didn't have to slam my door. You alright?"

Cameron shot him the bird.

"Man, fuck you!" the driver said. "I'm giving you a 1-star rating!" The driver sped away.

"I should have just driven my Benz," Cameron said under his breath.

Standing on the sidewalk, Cameron looked around and scoffed. He hated the suburbs. Who the hell would want to live out here? Cameron preferred his penthouse in the city, near all the good food and nightlife.

Pulling out his phone, Cameron checked the address. The house number was 632, which was posted on the mailbox. With that confirmed, he looked again at Ruby's previous text. The picture. Those three women and their sexy, naked bodies. He bit his lip and looked up at the house. The porch light of the two-story house was on, obviously as a courtesy to him. Cameron adjusted his shirt collar and unfastened another button, exposing more of his toned chest. He ran his hands through his hair, exhaled, and knocked.

A brief silence, then, "It's unlocked."

Cameron grabbed the doorknob and twisted, but it didn't budge. He tried again and pushed. Still nothing.

"It's locked!"

More silence. Cameron rolled his eyes.

"You can come in!" the woman shouted from inside.

Cameron huffed. How stupid could she be? The door was locked! Shaking his head, Cameron went to turn the knob again.

The door opened.

He squinted his eyes. He hadn't heard anyone approach. No clicks of the lock turning on the other side. Strange. He pushed the door all the way open and entered.

The lights were dim throughout the house. Beyond the entryway appeared to be a living room. To his right was a dining room with a table large enough to seat ten people, a chandelier above. A door in the dining room led into the kitchen. Cameron only took one step towards the living room before a woman appeared, moving around the corner from the kitchen. He froze.

Cameron noticed her blonde hair, curling past her shoulders. With the name Ruby, he'd expected a redhead. That was fine—he preferred blondes anyway, and wasn't surprised he'd previously hooked up with her, though he still didn't remember her. But she wore a scarlet dress that matched her name, its thigh-high slit and plunging neckline leaving little to the imagination. She smiled as she swayed her hips over to Cameron.

"You're here," she said. "I can't tell you how glad I am that you answered my text."

Okay, so it's definitely Ruby.

Cameron smiled. "Same here. Glad to be here."

She put her hands on his neck and planted a kiss on his lips. As soft as her lips were, he hissed as her hands landed on the place where the bitch at the club had bitten him.

"You okay?" she asked, pulling away. Before he could say anything, she noticed the bite on his neck. "Oh God, what happened?"

He covered the bite with his hand. "It's fine, really."

"You sure? I can get you a—"

He raised his free hand, trying to hold back his frustration. "Really, I'm okay."

Cameron looked around and past Ruby. Where were the other two women? This better not be some sort of trick. Ruby was hot, no doubt. Super-hot. But so were a slew of women back at the club, including the hottie at the bar. He'd dragged his ass to the suburbs for a foursome.

Ruby hesitated, then nodded. A smile grew on her lips, and she flicked her hair out of her face.

"I don't know if you're hungry or thirsty, but if not, I was thinking we could just go upstairs."

He smiled ear to ear. "Upstairs sounds good."

She took his hand. "That's good. Because I think you're going to need all the energy you've got." Ruby turned, giving him a lingering view of her curvy backside, and led him up the stairs.

Sweat collected on Cameron's brow as he watched her hips sway, the silky dress conforming to her curves. The upstairs lay in near darkness as she led him up another short staircase and opened a door at the end of the hall.

She pulled him ahead of her and into the room, where two silhouettes stood on the far side of the dark space. Only moonlight and streetlights from outside provided him with any sense of them being there.

The door shut behind, and Ruby's hand landed on his buttocks, moving around to his front as she slid around his body.

"We're so glad you accepted our invitation."

Ruby's first kiss came hard and fast. Her tongue slid into his mouth, colliding with his in a wave, and her hands slipped inside his open shirt.

How the hell could he not remember her? Her face had been familiar, but at some point, all hot blondes looked the same. But with her being this aggressive and this good of a kisser, it surprised Cameron he didn't have any memory of her.

Ruby moved her hands from out of his shirt to the buttons. She undid them slowly, pressing herself against him, the silk of her dress covering her breasts tickling his chest.

With the last button unfastened, a second set of hands wrapped around him, caressing his stomach. This woman's hands slid under his open shirt and pulled it over his shoulders and down his arms, removing it.

The mystery woman's hot breath hit the nape of his neck as Ruby kissed him again. At the same time, the woman behind him slid her tongue across the back of his neck to the top of his shoulder, giving it a single kiss. Then another. And another. Her hands moved down his stomach to the waistband of his pants, her fingertips sliding under them and causing him to lean his head back and moan, while Ruby scratched his pecs with her long nails.

"Aren't you glad you came over?" Ruby asked.

Cameron could hardly find the simple words to answer. "Oh, yeah."

She moved her face towards his left ear. "Your night has only begun."

Then, she and the mystery woman kissed, their lips smacking right next to his ear.

One of Ruby's hands slid down to the waistband of Cameron's pants, and she pulled him away. She led him to another area of the room and shoved his chest. Cameron fell back onto a bed. He laughed, giddy like a child.

Ruby slithered onto the bed and on top of him. Her hair tickled his stomach and chest as she slid up his body. From Cameron's left, the other woman who'd been seducing him got on the bed, and the third woman arrived on his right. Was this really happening?

Ruby licked his lips, then bit his bottom one. Unlike the bite at the club earlier, he invited it. Ruby wasn't gentle, but she clearly wasn't trying to harm him—only to turn him on. Then, she full-on kissed him, grinding her hips over his waist. Cameron leaned his head back and briefly closed his eyes, soaking in all the ecstasy.

He opened his eyes again when Ruby sat up, scratching Cameron's chest and stomach with her long nails. Her fingers landed under the waistband of his pants, and she unfastened his belt. At the same time, the mystery women on either side of him took hold of his arms. Almost simultaneously, they each took one of his fingers into their mouths and sucked. Cameron was throbbing now as Ruby pulled off his pants and boxer shorts, leaving him lying there naked.

Cameron then felt something metal clasp onto his left wrist, then his right. Another two clicks came, and when he tried to move his arms, he couldn't. He grinned.

"Handcuffs, huh?"

"I told you your night was only beginning," Ruby said, her fingernails teasing him by running across his waistline.

The women moved to the foot of the bed and shackled his ankles. Sweat trickled off Cameron's brow, and he closed his eyes, letting it happen. Not because he was giving up control, but because he was letting them think *they* held power over him. That was part of the fun.

Ruby scooted up, and Cameron felt the warmth between her legs, steaming on his manhood. He felt her skin, as she wasn't wearing underwear, and she hovered right over the top of him.

"You want me to sit all the way down, don't you?" Ruby asked.

"So fucking badly," Cameron said. He thrusted up, but she lifted herself, also pushing him back down.

"No, no," she said. "We're in control here. Not you. And if you want what we're here to give you, you're going to have to play by our rules."

Cameron licked his lips. "Oh yeah? And what are your rules?"

The women on either side ran their hands down Cameron's arms towards his shoulders. Their fingertips crawled up his neck, and Ruby pressed down on his stomach to steady herself over him as her heat continued to radiate down between his legs. She moaned, sliding her hands up his chest again and following the momentum to lean down to his face again. By the time she got there, the two other women were breathing into his ears.

"The rules are simple," Ruby whispered, only inches from Cameron's face. "All you have to do is listen to us."

"Really? That's it?" Cameron chortled. "Fuck, I can listen to you. What do you wanna talk about?"

He waited in anticipation, the women on either side still breathing into his ears. Ruby's fingernails glided up and down his side as she remained close to his face.

"I wanna talk about how you told me you'd call, but I was still bleeding when you left," a soft voice said into his right ear.

Cameron's smile collapsed. His eyebrows squeezed together.

"What?"

Ruby sat up. Her hands slid up to his chest, and she dug her nails into his skin, scraping down towards his stomach. Cameron jerked.

"Ouch!"

Ruby laid her palms on his stomach. "You're supposed to be listening!"

Cameron lifted his head off the pillow. The scratches burned, and blood trickled down his skin. Then, another gentle voice spoke, this time into his left ear.

"You said you were different," she said. "Then, you filmed it."

"Filmed it?" Cameron pulled against the restraints, looking to his left. "What the fuck are you talking about?"

Ruby guided her hand between Cameron's legs. Despite the strange suggestions, he was still hard. Her nails grazed his shaft, causing him to moan, and she moved her hand farther down to his swollen testicles. She tickled them sensually, leaning down towards his mouth again.

"Are you ready to listen to what I have to say now?" Ruby asked.

Cameron swallowed. "I ... I don't know. This is all so confusing. I don't know what's going on."

"The game is almost over," she said. "All you have to do is listen to me."

His breath hitched. "Okay." His voice cracked. "I'll listen."

Now, Ruby's fingers rested on his testicles. She breathed a hot, heavy breath on his neck, her lips brushing against it.

"You fucked me full of pain," she said. "Then called it a good time."

She squeezed his testicles lightly. It caught Cameron off-guard and he gasped, but it also made his cock flick back in pleasure.

"You planted something inside me, but then you ran away before it took root."

Ruby squeezed harder. Cameron hissed.

"You're hurting me," he said.

"Oh?" she asked. "What a coincidence."

Cameron thrashed against the restraints. "Let me go. I want out of here. Now!"

"You left me carrying more than just your lies," Ruby continued. "And you were the first man to make me feel like a woman, and the first to make me wish I wasn't one."

"What the fuck are you talking about?"

"I named her, you know," Ruby said. "Your daughter, that is." She sat up, pulling away from his face. "But you're never going to know her name. Never see her face. Never know what she sounds like, what she likes to do, what her favorite song or movie is. Because you don't deserve it. You don't deserve a goddamn thing."

Cameron's mind raced. He thrashed hard against the restraints, trying to break free, but also forgetting for a moment the grip Ruby had on his balls. He had to stop pulling so hard because it shot a pain up through him.

"Please," he said. "I don't know what I did to any of you, but I promise I'll make it right. Name your price."

A silence filled the room before all three women laughed in unison. A smile crept up on Cameron's face, and he joined in, laughing with them. Maybe he was on his way out of this mess.

"We don't want your money," Ruby said.

Cameron's throat tightened. "What do you want, then?"

She leaned down again, her breath blowing right into his face. "Everything else."

Ruby squeezed his testicles hard, and Cameron screamed. It felt like they might burst or pop right through the skin. He'd never felt so much pain in his life. Tears filled his eyes, rolling down his cheek.

"Stop," he said. "Please."

"Why should she stop?" the woman on the right asked.

"After everything you've done, you deserve this and much more," the woman on the left added.

Why were they doing this? Through the pain, Cameron searched his mind for who these women were. The truth was, he had lied to a lot of women. Probably wronged a lot of women, at least in their eyes. But he'd never intentionally tried to hurt anyone—he simply didn't want to settle down. He had too much going for that. Had too much—

"Oh, fuck!" Cameron screamed as Ruby dug her nails into his scrotum.

A nail punctured the skin, and Cameron felt on the verge of passing out.

Then, Ruby stopped. And though it hurt and burned and pounded, Cameron cried in relief. The weight of all three women lifted off the bed as they stood.

"Please, let me go," he gasped. "I'm sorry for whatever I did to you."

Heels clicked across the floor, and the lights came on.

Cameron blinked rapidly. He lifted his head and, beyond his almost naked body, he saw the three women standing there. Like Ruby, the other two women wore sexy dresses—the kind you'd wear out to a Michelin-starred steakhouse.

Ruby stood in the middle. With the lights on now and getting a better look, Cameron still didn't recognize her. Clearly, he'd wronged her, and he thumbed through his memories, trying to think about what she'd meant by, "You fucked me full of pain, then called it a good time."

A woman with darker blonde hair stood at her left. She had the biggest breasts of the three women, accentuated by the plunging black dress they poured out of. Her eyes were sharp with cat-eye makeup. The kind meant to kill, not to flirt. Like with Ruby, Cameron couldn't place her.

The caramel-skinned woman on Ruby's right did look familiar—probably because she wasn't his usual type. He mostly hooked up with white women. But occasionally he'd venture out and sleep with a Black or Latino or Asian woman. This woman's curly hair came to her shoulders, draping over a golden satin dress that highlighted her beautiful skin. Cameron thought he might actually remember her name. He narrowed his eyes, studying her.

"Jasmine?" he guessed.

The woman crossed her arms and raised an eyebrow, stealing a glance at Ruby and laughing. "Well, I'll be damned." Jasmine moved her hands to her hips. "You *do* remember at least one of us."

And he should have remembered her. Because Cameron had used his camera to film the two of them having sex and sent the video around to his friends. It had never ended up on the internet—at least, as far as he knew—but it had apparently ended up in the hands of someone who knew Jasmine. The moment she'd texted him about it, Cameron had blocked her number and her social media accounts.

"Oh, shit," he mumbled.

Because he really had hurt these women. Whether or not he'd remembered it, it had happened.

"I'm so sorry. Really. I didn't mean to hurt anybody."

The dark blonde crossed her arms, and Cameron noticed how the action pushed up her large breasts.

She laughed. "Look how pathetic you are—lying on the bed, crying like that."

"You're broken," Jasmine added.

Ruby took two steps forward. "And we're going to make sure you stay broken forever, and assure that forever is eternal."

Cameron tensed, his throat dry. "What the hell are you talking about?"

Glancing over her left shoulder, Ruby said, "Let her in, Chelsea."

The dark blonde strutted to a set of double doors behind her. As Cameron watched, he looked down to see the blood trickling down his stomach. His testicles still ached. Chelsea opened the doors, and a figure walked out of the bathroom.

Cameron squinted his eyes. He recognized her instantly.

"Tara?"

It was the woman from the club earlier that night. The one he'd planned to take home and fuck—until she'd bitten his neck, ruining their night together. She'd changed out of her halter top and leather pants into a black jumpsuit. Her dark hair, streaked with red, hung down.

The woman scoffed. "You can't even remember the fake name I gave you, but it doesn't matter. It's actually Lilia."

Cameron racked his brain. "But I just met you tonight. I haven't done anything to you. Fuck, you nearly bit a chunk out of my neck!"

Lilia laughed. "You're right that you have done nothing directly to me. But that doesn't matter. You've done your share to others, and I'm here to help remedy that. And that little bite? That was only because I had to taste you—to make sure you were the one I was looking for."

Cameron's arms and legs quivered. His brow furrowed.

"Remedy what? How?"

Ruby turned to a chest of drawers behind them. She opened the top one, and both Chelsea and Jasmine joined her. They each reached inside.

When they turned around, all three women held a unique item in their hands. Ruby held a small pairing knife. A pair of tongs rested in Jasmine's hand. And Chelsea grasped a spoon.

Cameron's eyes popped wide open. He bucked hard against his restraints, trying to break his legs or his arms loose. The metal tore into his wrists and ankles, but he didn't care.

The three women moved towards the bed, Lilia following closely behind.

"Stay away from me! Let me go!" Cameron looked around. "Help! Someone, help me!"

But he knew he was alone. Despite that, he strained to break free. Chelsea and Jasmine went to the left side of the bed, and Ruby and Lilia moved to the right. Cameron's heart crashed against his rib cage. Sweat soured his brow. He felt like he might piss himself.

"Hold him down," Jasmine said.

Cameron hyperventilated. "You don't have to do this! I'll pay you! Please, just let me go!"

Lilia pinned down his left shoulder, Chelsea his right. Then, Ruby appeared over his face, smiling down at him while Jasmine straddled him.

"Any last words?" Ruby asked.

"You fucking bitch! Let me go!" He spit in her face.

She didn't even bother to wipe it off. Ruby simply smiled and pinched his nose closed, forcing him to open his mouth to breathe.

When he did, Jasmine shoved the tongs into his mouth. His eyes went wide again as they clasped his tongue, filling his mouth with a metallic taste. He struggled to find air for his lungs. She pulled up, stretching his tongue out of his mouth. The pain was instant, a white-hot sensation radiating through his mouth and into his skull.

Then, with her fingers still pinching his nose closed and forcing Cameron to keep his mouth open, Ruby guided the knife towards his captured tongue.

For the final time, Cameron let out a scream that wasn't a wet, distorted mess.

The tongue came out quickly. It took Ruby only a couple of saws to get a cut going, and then she slit all the way across, detaching the muscle from Cameron's mouth forever.

It hung from the end of the tongs, a twitching and bleeding muscle like a worm, still pulsing and freshly detached from its base.

With a laugh, Jasmine tossed the tongs over her shoulder along with his severed tongue. She then switched places with Chelsea. The women held him down, and Chelsea raised an eyebrow, her cat-eye makeup prominent.

"You'll never see anything beautiful ever again," she said.

He tried to scream, but what came out was a wet gargle, bubbling into a choke. So much blood had collected in the back of his throat.

Ruby tugged his left eyelid open.

Chelsea leaned down and plunged the spoon into his left eye. Digging. And digging. The pain was so intense, Cameron teetered on the edge of consciousness. He choked while trying not to pass out as the vision in his left eye went black.

Next, Chelsea dug into his right eye, and his vision was gone forever.

Cameron let go then. He couldn't see. Couldn't talk or scream. He only felt the intensifying pain and heard the squishing sounds and the women cackling as they mutilated him. All was useless—any movement or fight, a fruitless stir.

When it was over, he lay blind and mute. He choked on the blood filling his throat. Someone shoved his face to the side, allowing him to empty his bloody mouth.

They don't want me to die.

A fingertip brushed over the wound on his neck where Lilia had bitten him earlier that night, causing him to jump. With two of his senses gone, his others heightened. He heard someone lean down toward his ear and smelled the distinct scent of lavender. The same perfume had permeated the club bathroom earlier that night.

"You know," Lilia said, "you were a good kisser, and you did taste good when I bit you. But I only had a small taste then. Had to make sure I knew who you were. And I couldn't turn you all the way—not until we mutilated you first. Had to make you appear like the monster you are before giving you my gift. Well, *curse*, in your case."

Curse? A taste? Turn me? What the fuck is she talking about?

He could barely think clearly, the blood running down his chin and cheeks.

"The good news, Cameron, is that you're going somewhere safe. A place where no woman will ever have to lay eyes on your disgusting face ever again. No one will find you. Rats might feed on you, and you'll feel the pain, but you will heal." She clicked her tongue. "And that's where the bad news comes in. Because you're going to live forever in this form, with no tongue. No eyes. No friends, money, fancy cars, or women to fuck and fuck over. You'll have nothing, and it'll last forever."

"Yuh...yuh cuh da dish!" Cameron said, hearing his tongueless voice for the first time. The women mocked him with their laughs.

"I thought of taking your hands," Lilia said, ignoring his pleas. "But it seems more fun to let you keep them. You'll think of all the women you fucked and you'll want to touch yourself, but the silver chains binding you won't allow it."

She hissed and then bit his neck again. This time, it was much harder, down into his jugular. She sucked, his blood squelching between her sharp teeth. It seemed to last for hours, and he faded to what had to be near death.

"I promise this is only the beginning," she said.

The last thing Cameron remembered before passing out was Lilia's passionate kiss as she spit a mouthful of blood down his throat, covering his mouth and pinching his nose until he swallowed the iron fluid.

How do you wake up when you can't open your eyes?

You can't, and you never will.

But it makes you see things more clearly, not being able to see the outside world.

Because all that remains are memories and regrets.

The future is like a sealed envelope in your mind—one that you can never open.

But it's there, just within reach.

Only, you have no way to grab it, chained up in this forbidden place.

No revenge.

No more lies.

Only infinite sadness.

Because no one is ever going to find you. Not down here. Not where they left you.

And for all your wrongdoings, the gift you received was an eternal life, but with no one to share it with and nothing to do but lie here and rot.

That's some real vigilante shit.

Who's Afraid of Little Old Me?

By Rebecca Rowland

Violet isn't her real name, not even close, but I called her Violet on the night we met, and it stuck.

"V and V," she responded, winking, her breath syrupy-sweet with the remnants of fermented alcohol. "Vickie, I can tell already: you and I are like those heavy-duty magnets. You know the ones?" Violet pointed her index and middle fingers toward each other, making the tips touch ever so slightly. "If you turn them face-down on the table, they will flip into a triple axel, or whatever that Tonya Harding move is—defy the very laws of physics—just to attach themselves to their partner."

"That level of attraction, huh?" I replied, pouring us each another surreptitious shot of mezcal from the bartender's stash.

"Those kinds of magnets, Vick?" She threw the alcohol to the back of her throat and continued. "Once they connect with one other, they never let go. Unless, you know, one begins to rot." She slid an American Spirit between her lips. "You understand."

I didn't, but we've been inseparable ever since.

She never asked me to move in. We met at that dive bar in late October, both having wandered into a concert for a local band. She took me home, to the shabby first floor of a broken-down house at the mouth of a dead-end street, and I never left.

The apartment is sparsely furnished, a bare-bones decorator job fit for a shoestring income. Neither of us go to work or school, but somehow, there is always orange juice in the refrigerator and vodka in the freezer and a Skittles rainbow of assorted pills scattered about the glass-topped coffee table.

A few times a week, strangers drop by, bringing greasy boxes of pizza or fragrant bags of fast food and I feel my stomach claw desperately at the spaces between the other organs in my abdominal cavity. Otherwise, I am content to curl up in our cozy stupor.

When Violet and I have sex, we are like rabid dogs. She digs her teeth into my shoulder and I yelp so loudly, I expect firemen to come bursting through the door, hoses in hands. One evening, Violet and I are lying in bed, the electric heater making a whirred cough as its fan pushes out warmth from behind layers of dust. I rub the tender skin just above my clavicle and pull the blanket over my naked torso while Violet sits up, her breasts resting heavy against the bottom of her ribcage.

"I'm going for a smoke," she says, swinging her legs to the edge of the bed. "Do you need anything?"

I don't, but I shimmy back into my clothes and follow her.

She falls heavily back on the sofa and paws about the coffee table for the television remote. When she presses a button, the once gray living room pulses with a pale blue glow, and from the speakers a nasally voice drones on about a body discovered beside a highway in an area of the country I never plan to see.

Violet's spine instantly straightens. She loves true crime shows, watches them like she's studying for a dissertation defense in forensic science. "Dental records," she says, echoing the narrator's mechanical explanation.

A photo of the victim pops up on the screen. She is bubblegum pretty. Blonde with heavily rouged cheeks and electric blue eyeliner. Her smile, a railroad track of silvery braces, is open and uninhibited, a tell-tale sign that she hasn't been crushed under the bitterness of adolescence yet. "She's just a kid," I say.

"Dumb ass," she mutters, ignoring my comment. She shakes her head at the newscaster fuzzy with soft focus. "If you're going to dump a body, you've got to burn off the fingertips, knock out some teeth. Maybe even saw off the extremities. Something to stall the investigation. Everyone knows that."

I nod in agreement, then glance warily about. "Do you ever worry about being broken into?" I ask. The faint light from a streetlamp peers through the naked windows, and my eyes return to Violet, to her bare breasts. "I mean, anyone could walk by and—"

Violet waves a hand dismissively at me, but her gaze remains fixed on the screen. "There's just the empty lot across the street, and most of the other houses are deserted."

I know she is telling the truth. I have not seen a neighbor the entire time I have been staying here, just the occasional transient who squats in the dilapidated Cape Cod next door. Every lot is overgrown, including Violet's. Dormant forsythia bushes flank the edges of the property line like skeletal sentries. An abandoned car, its tires and VIN tags pried from its body and shiny electronics removed, is a permanent statue at the end of the block, one discarded victim successfully stripped of its identity.

"Hardly anyone comes around here," she continues and frowns. "Except you." Violet turns to me. Her face is stony, then melts into mischievousness. "Are *you* a secret harbinger of death and destruction?" she asks, winking.

I smile weakly, then look back at the windows. I am certain I see a dark shape darting sideways behind the glass.

"Besides," she states confidently, "everybody likes me."

"I like myself when I am drinking," I whisper. "It's everyone else who has a problem with me."

"What did you say?" Violet asks.

"Nothing."

Violet leans forward and reaches her hand across the coffee table again, her fingers dancing like a fleshy spider until they land on a pair of green and ivory-colored capsules. Without examining them closely, she tosses one at me and the other into her mouth like popcorn kernels.

"Tony left some of his Librium," she explains.

Tony is a regular visitor to the apartment, though the nature of their relationship is unclear. When our coffee table pharmacy wanes, Violet sends him a quick text, and there he is, supplies replenished. Sometimes, Violet disappears into the bedroom with him after a particularly generous delivery. Our very own Subscribe n' Save service.

Violet picks up a plastic bottle half-full of water and unscrews the cap. "It's times like these that we really need to chill out," she says, taking a swig. "You understand."

I don't, but she does not offer me the bottle, so I say nothing and toss the pill into the back of my throat. It tumbles awkwardly, scratching dryly down my esophagus, and it is only then I realize that neither of us has eaten since breakfast.

Violet lights a cigarette, and it's as if the whole room immediately fills with smoke.

There is a soft tap at the door, but when I stand to answer it, Violet frowns again; this time, with confusion. "Where are you going?" she asks.

I glance at the door, then back at Violet. I bite my lower lip. "To bed," I say quickly. "I can't sleep out here."

I turn and leave the room before she can protest, before whatever is at the door can come inside.

The next morning, I stumble from the bedroom to find Violet's attention rapt on the coffee table, her hand making a high-pitched tapping noise as she frantically chops at a pile of white powder with a razor blade.

"We're out of coffee," she explains.

We don't drink coffee.

I turn on the television and click the tiny remote until I find a streaming service sailing along a Möbius strip of *Three's Company* episodes. Violet places a disarticulated piece of a fast-food straw up to one nostril, covers the other with her middle finger, and inhales a line. When she wordlessly hands the red and white tube to me, I see there are teeth marks imprinted on one end, and they remind me of Violet biting my shoulder during sex. A part of me is aroused; another part is frightened.

I place the straw at the beginning of one line and before I can blink, the cocaine is sizzling along the synapses of my brain like bacon on a griddle.

"Who chewed on you?" I ask, tossing the straw a solid side-eye before aligning it against my other nostril. Violet only rubs her nose and snorts.

A half hour later, I am no longer curious about the bite mark perpetrator; I am completely engrossed in solving the mystery.

"Who was it that came over on Sunday?" I ask, a small notepad I've commandeered from the kitchen junk drawer sitting in one hand, a nearly empty Bic ballpoint poised expectantly in the other. Suddenly, I am the Cagney to Violet's Lacey, or one of the other technicolor detectives in the shows that stream ad nauseam on our television. "Ron? Ian? Henry? Roger?"

I know no one with those names, but my mind is racing a mile a minute, and my mouth is panting too heavily to catch up.

"Yes," Violet says. She runs a knuckle back and forth under her top lip.

My hands are trembling, and as I grasp them together to steady myself, I drop the pen and paper onto the scratchy, beige carpet. On the television screen, Jack Tripper pulls one of his blonde roommates to his chest and squeezes.

Violet juts her chin toward their embrace. "Isn't that the actress with three nipples?"

I frown. "Priscilla Barnes?"

Violet rubs her nose, then waves me back over to the table. "Yeah. Yeah, yeah," she repeats. "I had a real thing for her back in high school."

"You went to high school with Priscilla Barnes?" This comes from Tony, whose presence I hadn't noticed until just that moment. He's wearing a ski cap with an enormous blue pom-pom poised atop. A dusting of fresh snow has almost completely melted into the crocheted fabric. I'm still bent over, the mysteriously masticated straw held up to my nostril again. I inhale two more lines as my eyes dart frantically about the room, wondering who else has slipped stealthily inside.

On the television, Jack Tripper stumbles over his own feet and tumbles down a set of stairs. The blue December sunlight streaking through the dirty windows dims slightly, like he's accidentally kicked some loose wiring in the sky on the way down.

Violet beats her palms softly against the couch cushion. "*Mallrats*," she says, and her non-sequitur is punctuated by the seventies sitcom laugh track, a tin can dumping out dead people's chuckles and guffaws. "It was the nineties. You understand."

I don't, but I am still hunched over the table, too fixated with trying to catch my breath to say so.

There is a metallic pop as Violet pulls the tab on a can of beer. "When did it get so hot in here?" she asks, then gulps audibly.

I right myself and walk much too quickly to the nearby recliner. It was once navy in color, faded now to a pale gray like our muted view of the outside world. Violet is right: the room feels like a sauna. Water simmers inside the nearby radiator, and the acid in my stomach gurgles a reply. I sink into the worn cushions and push backwards until I am staring at the ceiling. My heart is dancing on a trampoline inside my ribcage, trying its best to leap higher and higher to palm slap the gritty finish of the gypsum plaster.

When I squint, the beads of sweat that dot my forehead dribble down into my eyes. I rub them and stare upwards again, but my heart beats so violently that it shakes my face, blurring my vision. Through the haze, I see the dark shape from behind the window slithering its way along the edges of the panes. It oozes between the caulk, skulks along the ceiling paint's nicotine stains, then shimmies and twirls until my eyes are cartwheeling and somersaulting just to keep up.

I blink rapidly to clear my vision and twist my head sideways. It is only then that I notice Violet's disappearance. Maybe that's not the word; Violet doesn't *disappear*. It's not an altogether absence but a creeping exit from my line of vision, random pieces of her fading away like the end of a song on a 1980s LP. The temporary dim from the day has settled in for the long winter, a gossamer overcast from the days growing shorter, but by the afternoon, the whole apartment is swaddled in a thick gray cloud and Violet herself appears nearly translucent.

"Violet?" I whisper, but neither she nor Tony acknowledge me. My lungs tighten. Panic washes over me.

On the television, Jack Tripper puts the final touches on a birthday cake, then staggers forward and lands face-first in the frosting.

I blink. When I open my eyes again, the world outside the windows is black. Violet stretches one arm toward the end table and switches on the lamp. If I listen close, I can hear the tiny filament on each incandescent bulb sizzling away. The room fills with a greenish-gold light, every inch except one corner within arm's reach where a dark shadow lurks.

I am certain it is the dark shadow from behind the window.

Tony is no longer in the room, and I'm not sure when he left.

"Did I nod off?" I ask. The question reverberates in my head, then bounces around the room, side-swiping Violet but missing its bullseye. I wonder if I have spoken it out loud but don't bother to repeat the question.

On the scratchy beige carpet is a small notepad, illegible scribbles covering the exposed page. Beside it rests half of a plastic straw, strangely familiar. I try to remember where I've seen it, but my head feels strange. I am certain there are painkillers scattered across the coffee table: Vicodin and Valium and Lorcet and Percocet, an assortment fit for Dr. Seuss's address book, but I am too exhausted to get up. My body feels rigid, pinned to the contours of the recliner.

Outside the sun rises, but its light breaks upon the windows and collapses like shed pine needles. Snow falls gently, and flakes drift against the glass, first sticking, then liquifying and streaming in rivulets.

I drift into a dreamless sleep, waking only once to see Violet has left to go to bed without me.

The dark shadow, however, remains vigilant beside me.

Jack Tripper is no longer on the television screen. In his place, Alice Hyatt slams the receiver of Mel's Diner's pay phone against a wall in frustration.

Tony is sitting on the couch, staring in my direction. He holds one hand over his nose and mouth like a makeshift infection mask.

On the screen, Flo Castleberry pats her orange bouffant then pulls Vera, the third waitress with a stomach full of sleeping pills, to her feet. Alice screams something about an ambulance not coming.

I tilt my head to my chest. There is something light-colored, the size of a small marble or a flower petal, sitting in a stomach fold of my t-shirt. A dark red stain like raspberry Kool-Aid saturates the fabric around it.

When I look up again, no one is on the couch. No one is in the room at all. Every lamp in the apartment burns full force. Somehow, however, the darkness in the corner has widened.

"Viole*nt*? Viole*nt*?" I try to shout her name, to ascertain if anyone is home, but the word comes out different, mushy, the edges of the final T soft and malleable. Wet, even. Carefully, I press my lips together. The top of my jaw overshoots the bottom and this puzzles me. I open my mouth and a dribble of fluid leaks out, spilling along my chin.

I look down at my torso once more. Upon second inspection, I see it clearly: the yellowed ivory item speckled with a crust of dried crimson. A tooth. My tooth. I run my tongue along the perimeter of my gums as my eyes drift to the coffee table. Alongside the kaleidoscope of pills and powders, more teeth are scattered—twenty or thirty, at least—alongside a pair of bloodied, rusty pliers.

"Vee?" I call, but it comes out only as a whisper. A watery, smacking whisper.

And then, she is next to me, curling her lithe body over mine in the recliner. Tony's blue pop-pom cap hides all her hair, and thick rubber gloves, the kind we use for washing dishes—in the rare instance when dishes need to be washed—cover her hands and forearms.

I try to meet her embrace, but my muscles do not respond.

I don't move. I can't move.

She lifts me out of the recliner, up up up, light as a feather, stiff as a board, and carries me like a new bride toward the threshold. My neck is too stiff to turn, but when Violet tilts my body slightly, I spy the familiar beige carpet, the cathode ray tube television, the pale gray-blue recliner.

The latter is dark with a damp, ugly stain the shape of a person, the upholstery soaked with decomposition now a holy shroud.

As we pass the wide shadow in the corner, it spreads its wings to caress me one last time, a melancholy farewell.

Under the gray flannel sky, the dense snow curls its bear paws around my arms and legs. Violet lays me, gently, in an unplowed bank hidden from the road in the lot across the street. Husks of wild grass tickle, then scratch my cheeks. I open my mouth to speak but the only thing circulating inside is icy air, my barren mouth just a tack board of membrane and open sores.

"I couldn't call the paramedics, and I can't risk calling the cops," Violet whispers in my ear. "There would be too many questions." She runs her skeletal hand down my face, shutting my eyelids, the last click of the light switch finally turning everything black.

"You understand."

And finally, as I feel her pile the snow and sand over my face, I do.

Quick Favor

Thank you so much for dedicating your time to reading this book! May we ask a quick favor?

Will you please take a moment to leave a review on Goodreads and wherever you purchased the book? Your words have power. Your review can help this book reach more readers. We appreciate you!

More great titles from Sobelo Books
available at www.SobeloBooks.com
and wherever books are sold.

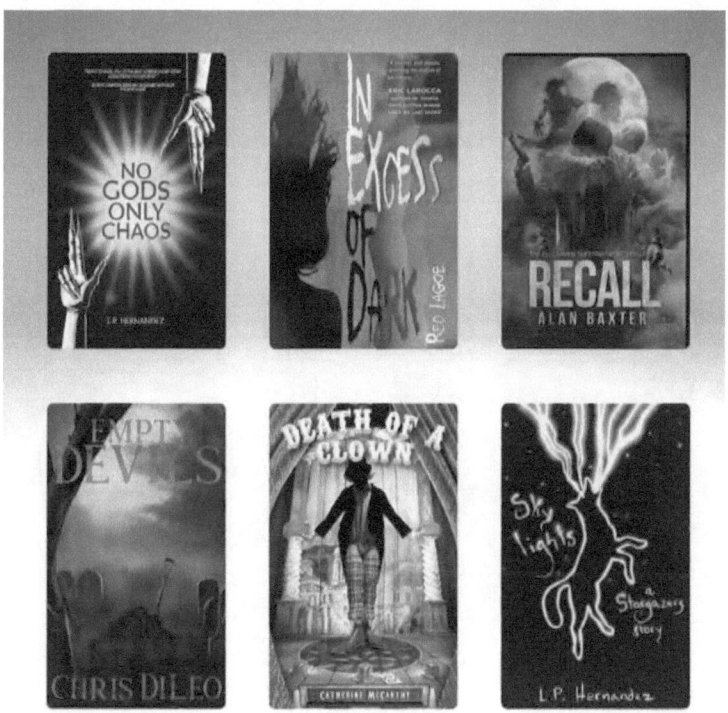

www.ingramcontent.com/pod-product-compliance
Lightning Source LLC
LaVergne TN
LVHW040053080526
838202LV00045B/3606